Disney
DuckTales

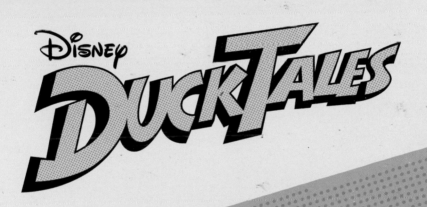

Facebook: **facebook.com/idwpublishing**
Twitter: **@idwpublishing**
YouTube: **youtube.com/idwpublishing**
Tumblr: **tumblr.idwpublishing.com**
Instagram: **instagram.com/idwpublishing**

ISBN: **978-1-68405-559-3**   22 21 20 19   1 2 3 4

COVER ARTIST
MARCO GHIGLIONE
and CRISTINA STELLA

COVER COLORIST
KAWAII STUDIO

LETTERER
TOM B. LONG

SERIES ASSISTANT EDITORS
ELIZABETH BREI
and ANNI PERHEENTUPA

SERIES EDITOR
CHRIS CERASI

COLLECTION EDITORS
JUSTIN EISINGER
and ALONZO SIMON

COLLECTION DESIGNER
CLYDE GRAPA

Originally published as DUCKTALES issues #15–17.

Chris Ryall, President, Publisher, & CCO

John Barber, Editor-In-Chief

Cara Morrison, Chief Financial Officer

Matt Ruzicka, Chief Accounting Officer

David Hedgecock, Associate Publisher

Jerry Bennington, VP of New Product Development

Lorelei Bunjes, VP of Digital Services

Justin Eisinger, Editorial Director, Graphic Novels & Collections

Eric Moss, Senior Director, Licensing and Business Development

Ted Adams and Robbie Robbins, IDW Founders

Special thanks to Stefano Ambrosio, Stefano Attardi, Julie Dorris, Marco
Ghiglione, Jodi Hammerwold, Behnoosh Khalili, Manny Mederos, Eugene
Paraszczuk, Carlotta Quattrocolo, Roberto Santillo, Christopher Troise,
and Camilla Vedove.

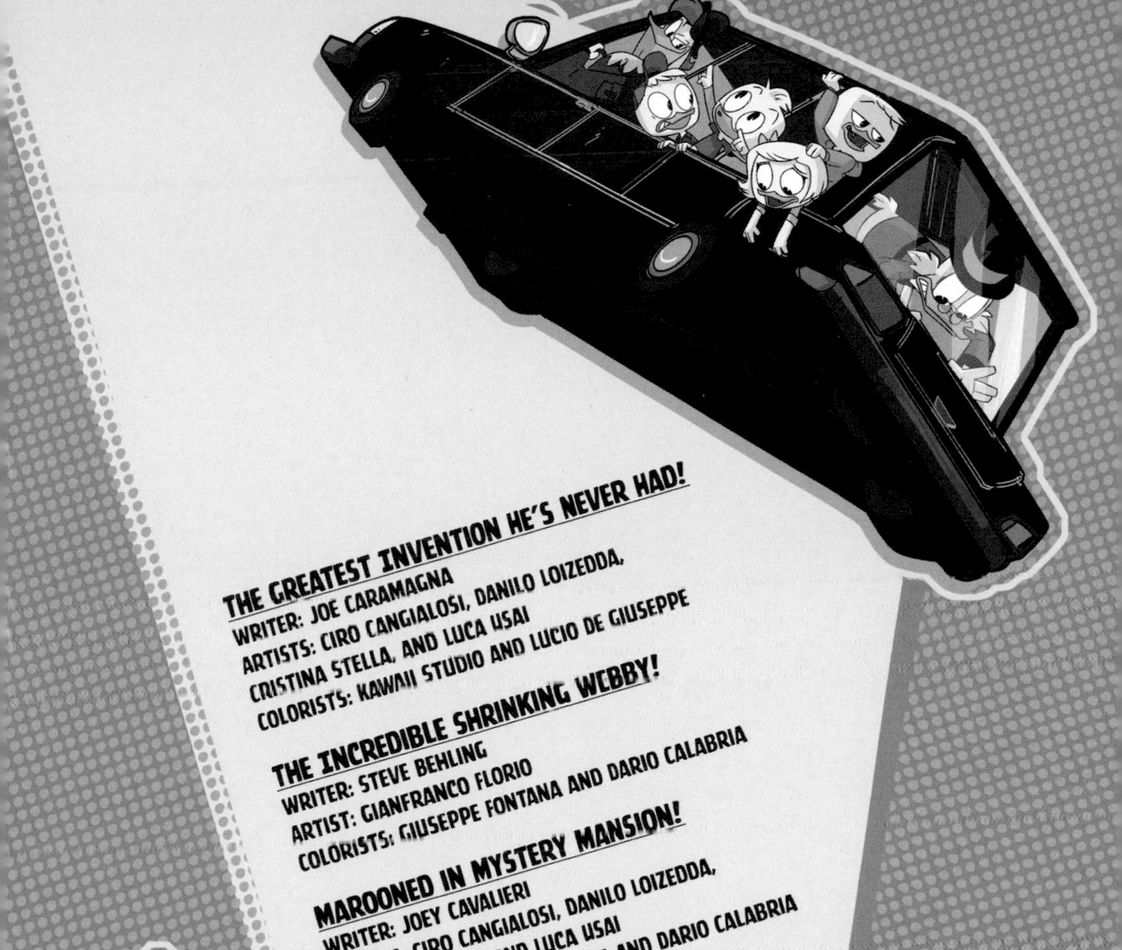

THE GREATEST INVENTION HE'S NEVER HAD!

WRITER: JOE CARAMAGNA
ARTISTS: CIRO CANGIALOSI, DANILO LOIZEDDA, CRISTINA STELLA, AND LUCA USAI
COLORISTS: KAWAII STUDIO AND LUCIO DE GIUSEPPE

THE INCREDIBLE SHRINKING WEBBY!

WRITER: STEVE BEHLING
ARTIST: GIANFRANCO FLORIO
COLORISTS: GIUSEPPE FONTANA AND DARIO CALABRIA

MAROONED IN MYSTERY MANSION!

WRITER: JOEY CAVALIERI
ARTISTS: CIRO CANGIALOSI, DANILO LOIZEDDA, CRISTINA STELLA, AND LUCA USAI
COLORISTS: GIUSEPPE FONTANA AND DARIO CALABRIA

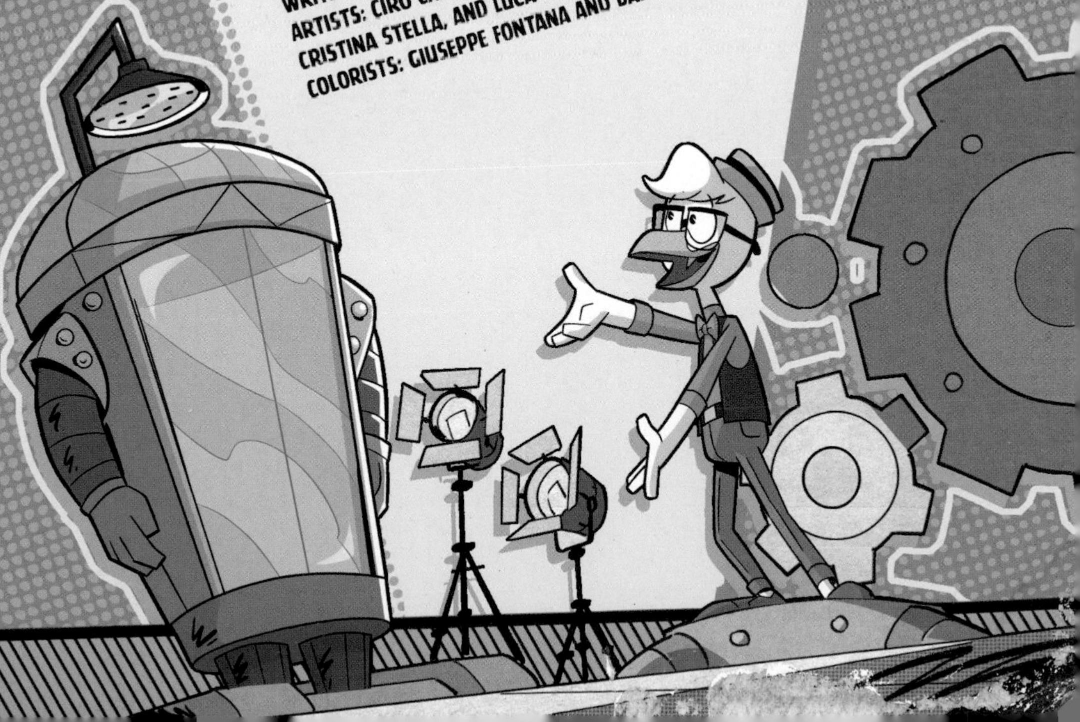

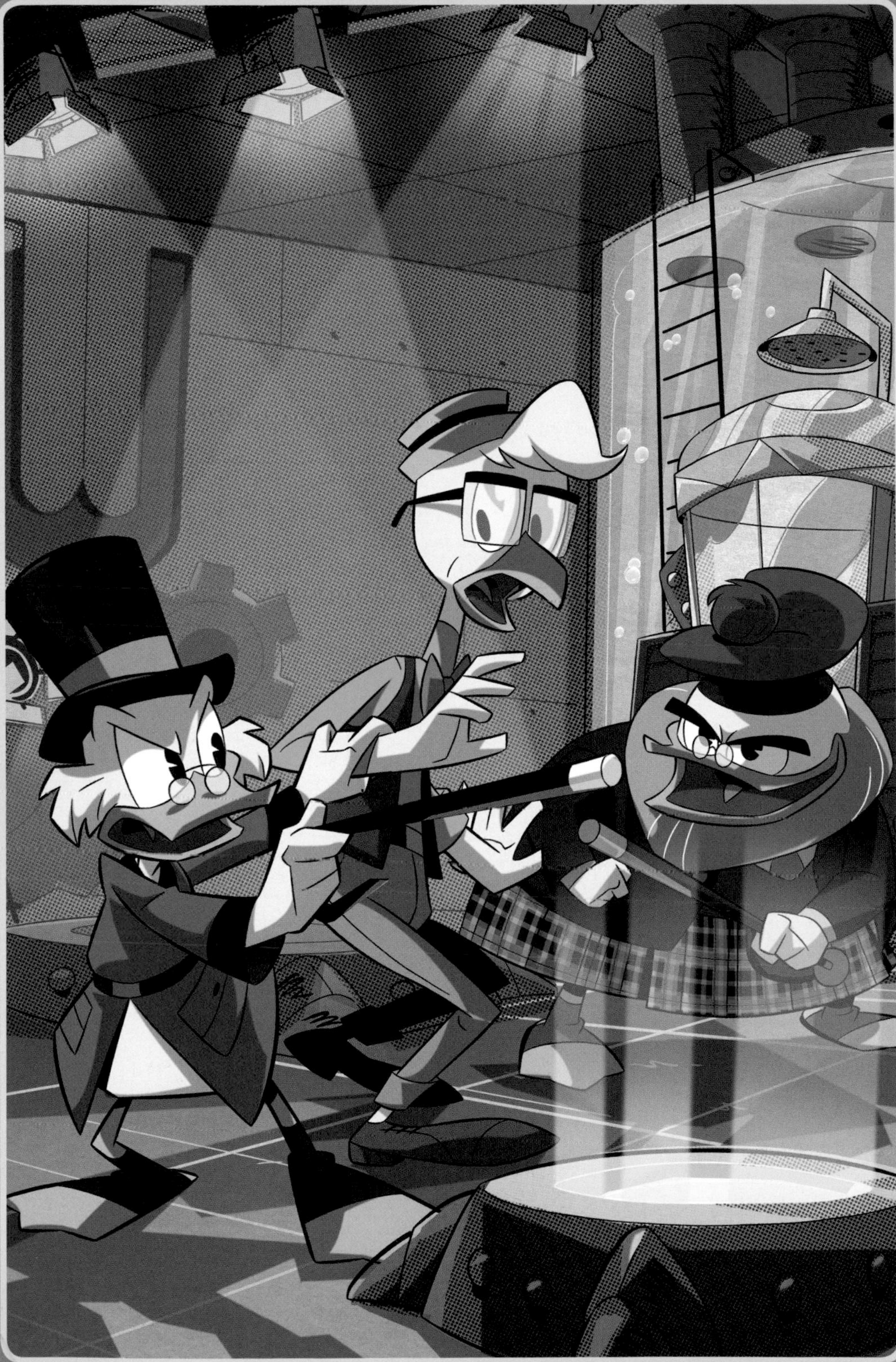

Art by Marco Ghiglione and Cristina Stella, Colors by Kawaii Studio

Disney DuckTales

THE GREATEST INVENTION HE'S NEVER HAD!

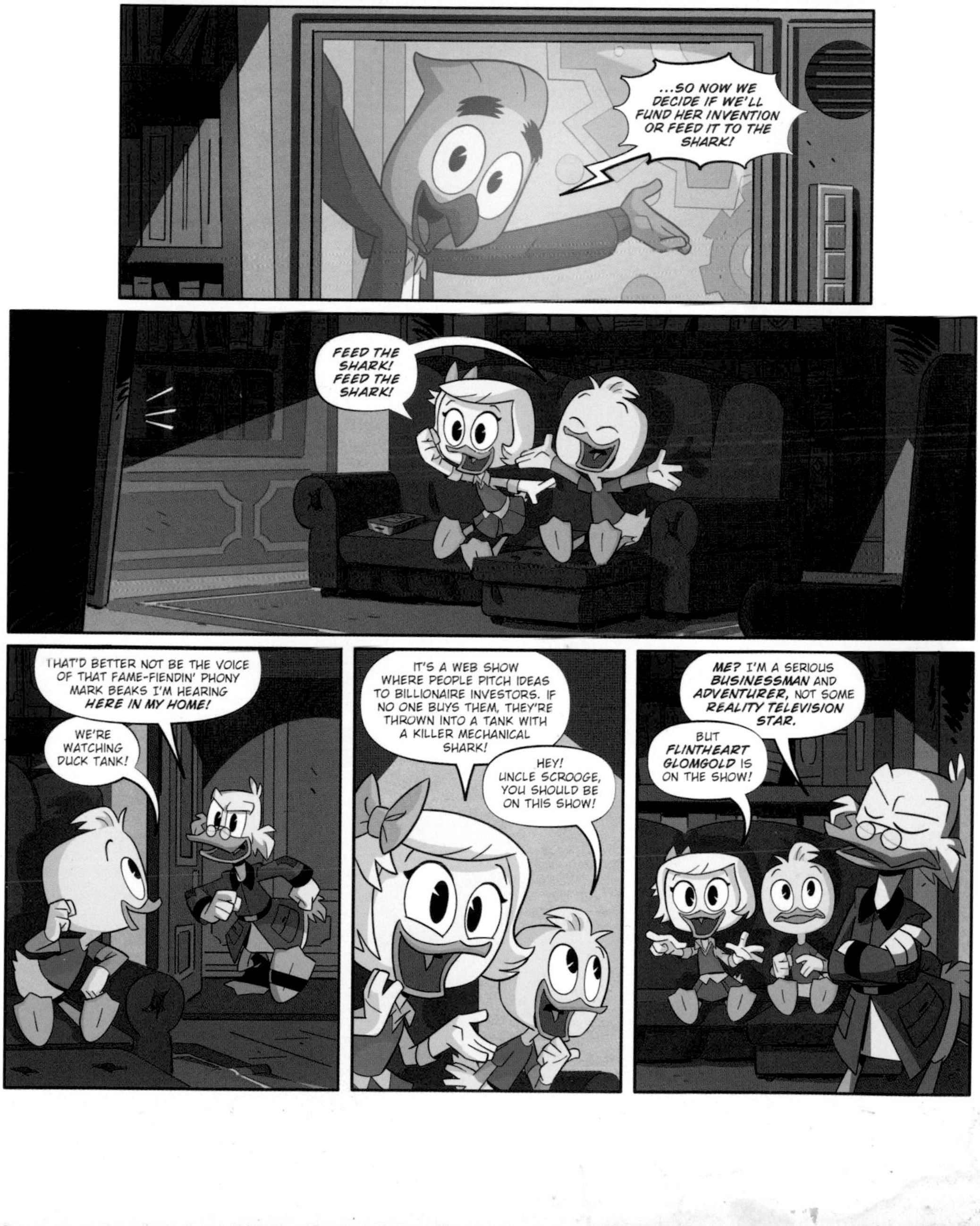
...SO NOW WE DECIDE IF WE'LL FUND HER INVENTION OR FEED IT TO THE SHARK!
FEED THE SHARK! FEED THE SHARK!
THAT'D BETTER NOT BE THE VOICE OF THAT FAME-FIENDIN' PHONY MARK BEAKS I'M HEARING HERE IN MY HOME!
WE'RE WATCHING DUCK TANK!
IT'S A WEB SHOW WHERE PEOPLE PITCH IDEAS TO BILLIONAIRE INVESTORS. IF NO ONE BUYS THEM, THEY'RE THROWN INTO A TANK WITH A KILLER MECHANICAL SHARK!
HEY! UNCLE SCROOGE, YOU SHOULD BE ON THIS SHOW!
ME? I'M A SERIOUS BUSINESSMAN AND ADVENTURER, NOT SOME REALITY TELEVISION STAR.
BUT FLINTHEART GLOMGOLD IS ON THE SHOW!

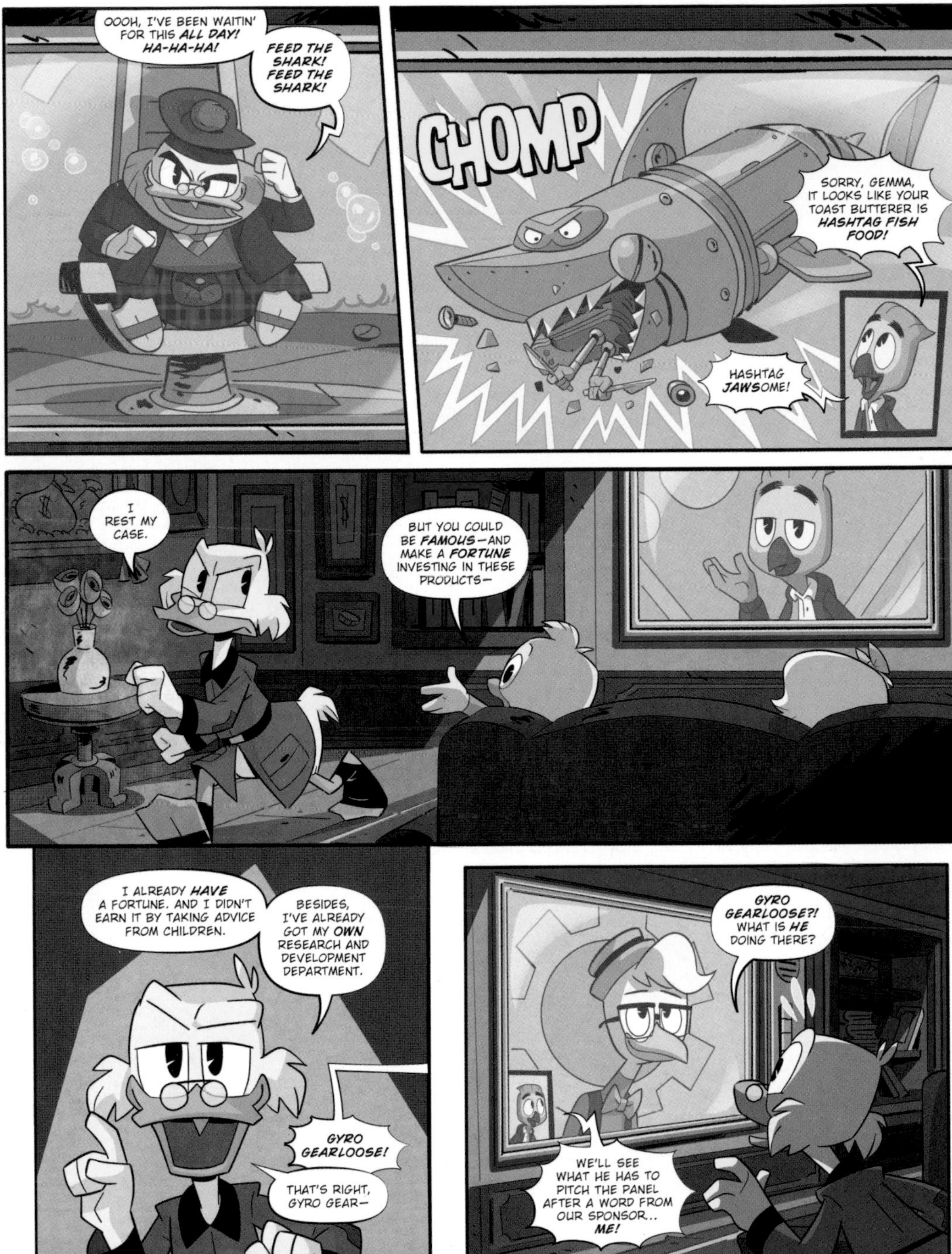
OOOH, I'VE BEEN WAITIN' FOR THIS ALL DAY! HA-HA-HA!
FEED THE SHARK! FEED THE SHARK!
CHOMP
SORRY, GEMMA, IT LOOKS LIKE YOUR TOAST BUTTERER IS HASHTAG FISH FOOD!
HASHTAG JAWSOME!
I REST MY CASE.
BUT YOU COULD BE FAMOUS—AND MAKE A FORTUNE INVESTING IN THESE PRODUCTS—
I ALREADY HAVE A FORTUNE. AND I DIDN'T EARN IT BY TAKING ADVICE FROM CHILDREN.
BESIDES, I'VE ALREADY GOT MY OWN RESEARCH AND DEVELOPMENT DEPARTMENT.
GYRO GEARLOOSE!
THAT'S RIGHT, GYRO GEAR—
GYRO GEARLOOSE?! WHAT IS HE DOING THERE?
WE'LL SEE WHAT HE HAS TO PITCH THE PANEL AFTER A WORD FROM OUR SPONSOR... ME!

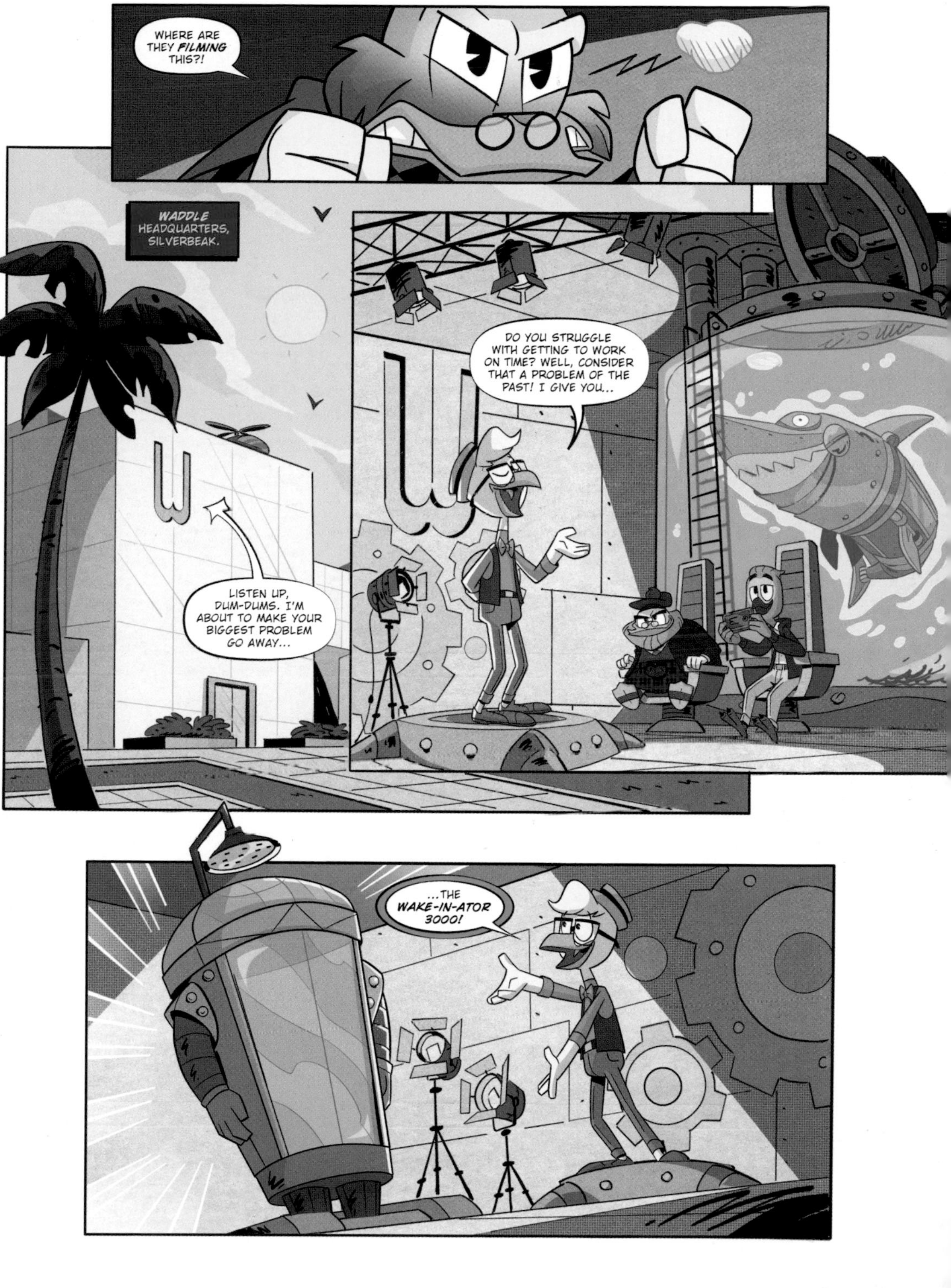
WHERE ARE THEY FILMING THIS?!
WADDLE HEADQUARTERS, SILVERBEAK.
LISTEN UP, DUM-DUMS. I'M ABOUT TO MAKE YOUR BIGGEST PROBLEM GO AWAY...
DO YOU STRUGGLE WITH GETTING TO WORK ON TIME? WELL, CONSIDER THAT A PROBLEM OF THE PAST! I GIVE YOU...
...THE WAKE-IN-ATOR 3000!

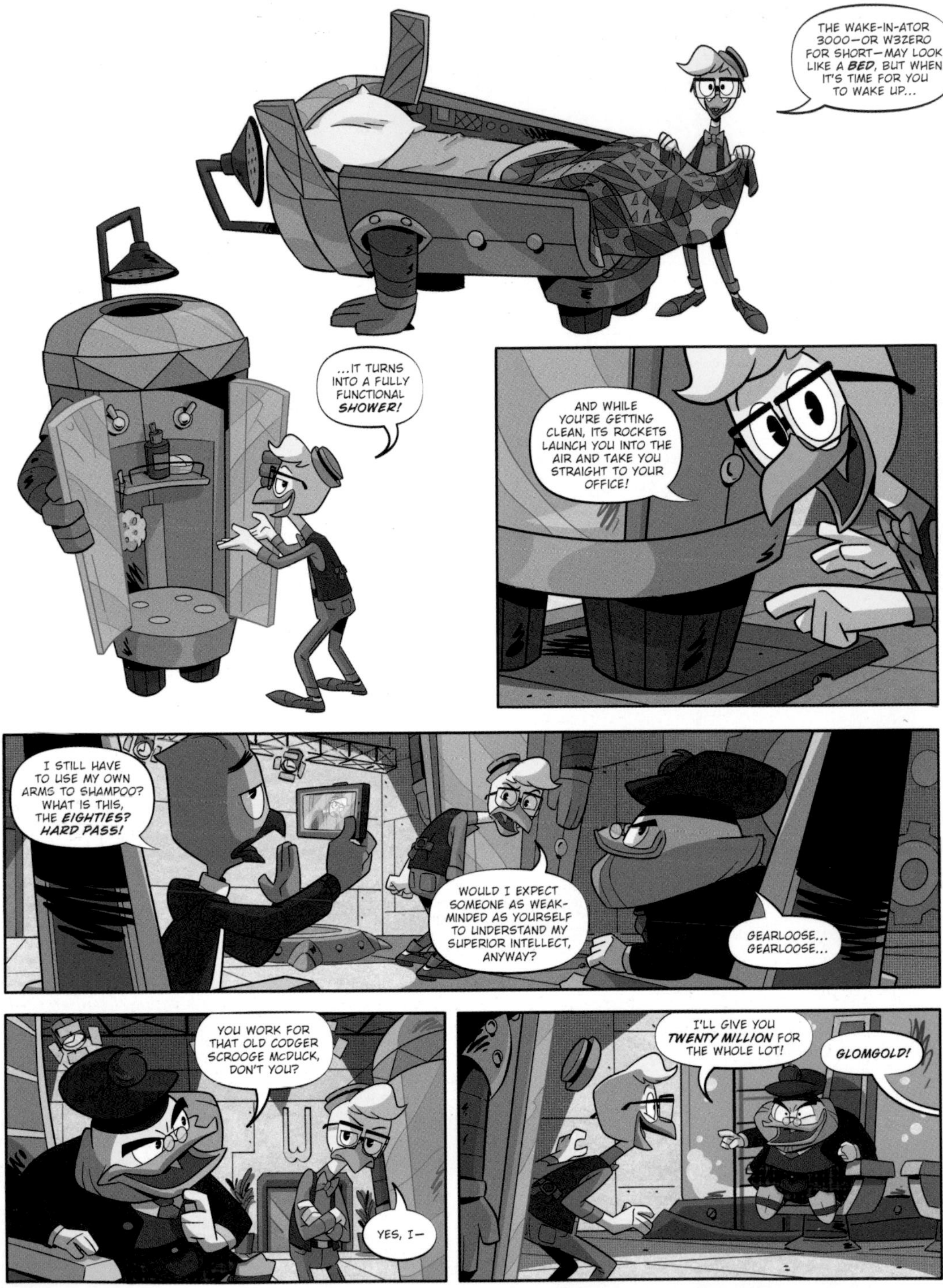
THE WAKE-IN-ATOR 3000—OR W3ZERO FOR SHORT—MAY LOOK LIKE A *BED*, BUT WHEN IT'S TIME FOR YOU TO WAKE UP...
...IT TURNS INTO A FULLY FUNCTIONAL *SHOWER!*
AND WHILE YOU'RE GETTING CLEAN, ITS ROCKETS LAUNCH YOU INTO THE AIR AND TAKE YOU STRAIGHT TO YOUR OFFICE!
I STILL HAVE TO USE MY OWN ARMS TO SHAMPOO? WHAT IS THIS, THE *EIGHTIES? HARD PASS!*
WOULD I EXPECT SOMEONE AS WEAK-MINDED AS YOURSELF TO UNDERSTAND MY SUPERIOR INTELLECT, ANYWAY?
GEARLOOSE... GEARLOOSE...
YOU WORK FOR THAT OLD CODGER SCROOGE McDUCK, DON'T YOU?
YES, I—
I'LL GIVE YOU *TWENTY MILLION* FOR THE WHOLE LOT!
GLOMGOLD!

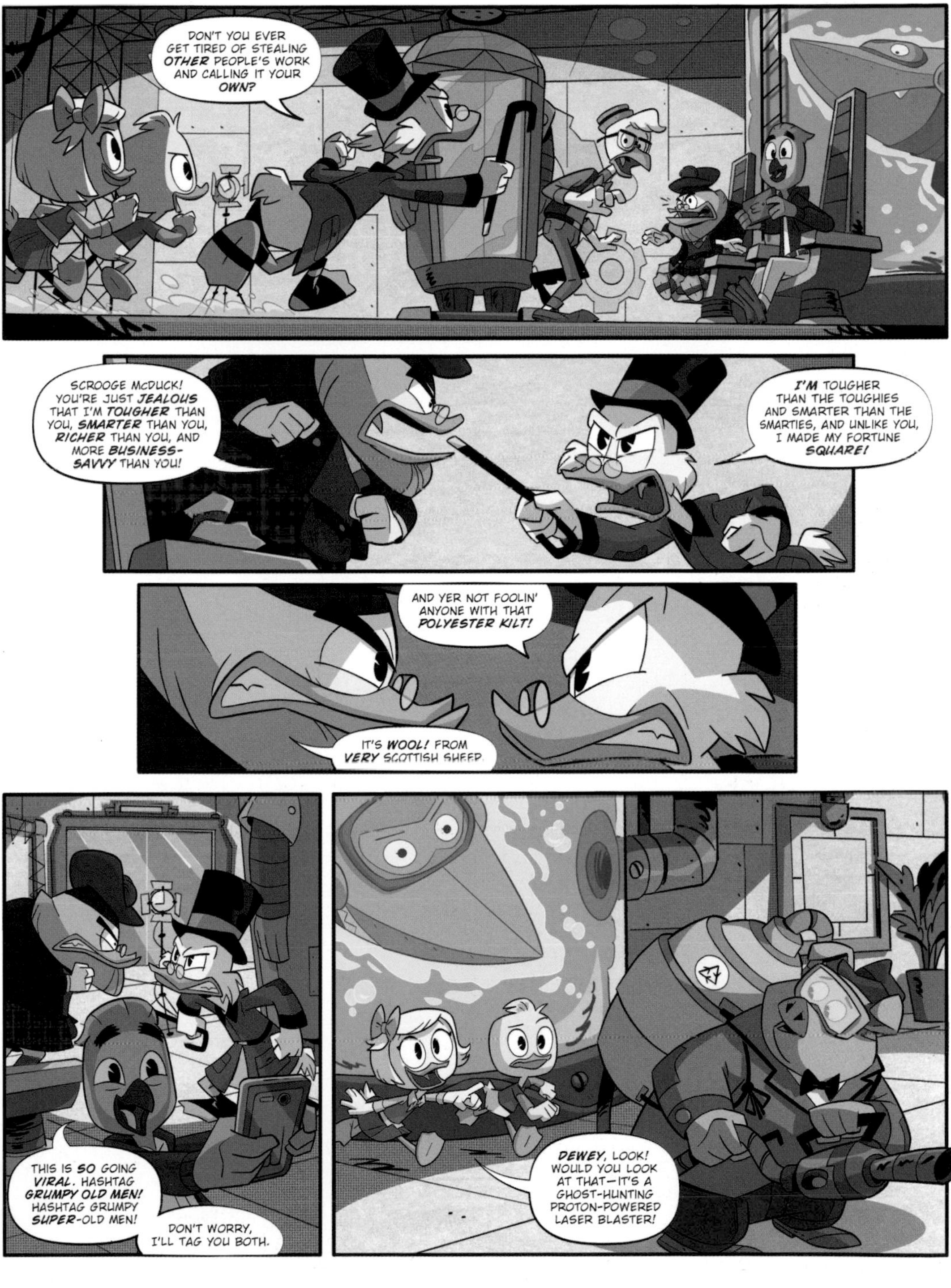
DON'T YOU EVER GET TIRED OF STEALING OTHER PEOPLE'S WORK AND CALLING IT YOUR OWN?
SCROOGE McDUCK! YOU'RE JUST JEALOUS THAT I'M TOUGHER THAN YOU, SMARTER THAN YOU, RICHER THAN YOU, AND MORE BUSINESS-SAVVY THAN YOU!
I'M TOUGHER THAN THE TOUGHIES AND SMARTER THAN THE SMARTIES, AND UNLIKE YOU, I MADE MY FORTUNE SQUARE!
AND YER NOT FOOLIN' ANYONE WITH THAT POLYESTER KILT!
IT'S WOOL! FROM VERY SCOTTISH SHEEP.
THIS IS SO GOING VIRAL. HASHTAG GRUMPY OLD MEN! HASHTAG GRUMPY SUPER-OLD MEN!
DON'T WORRY, I'LL TAG YOU BOTH.
DEWEY, LOOK! WOULD YOU LOOK AT THAT—IT'S A GHOST-HUNTING PROTON-POWERED LASER BLASTER!

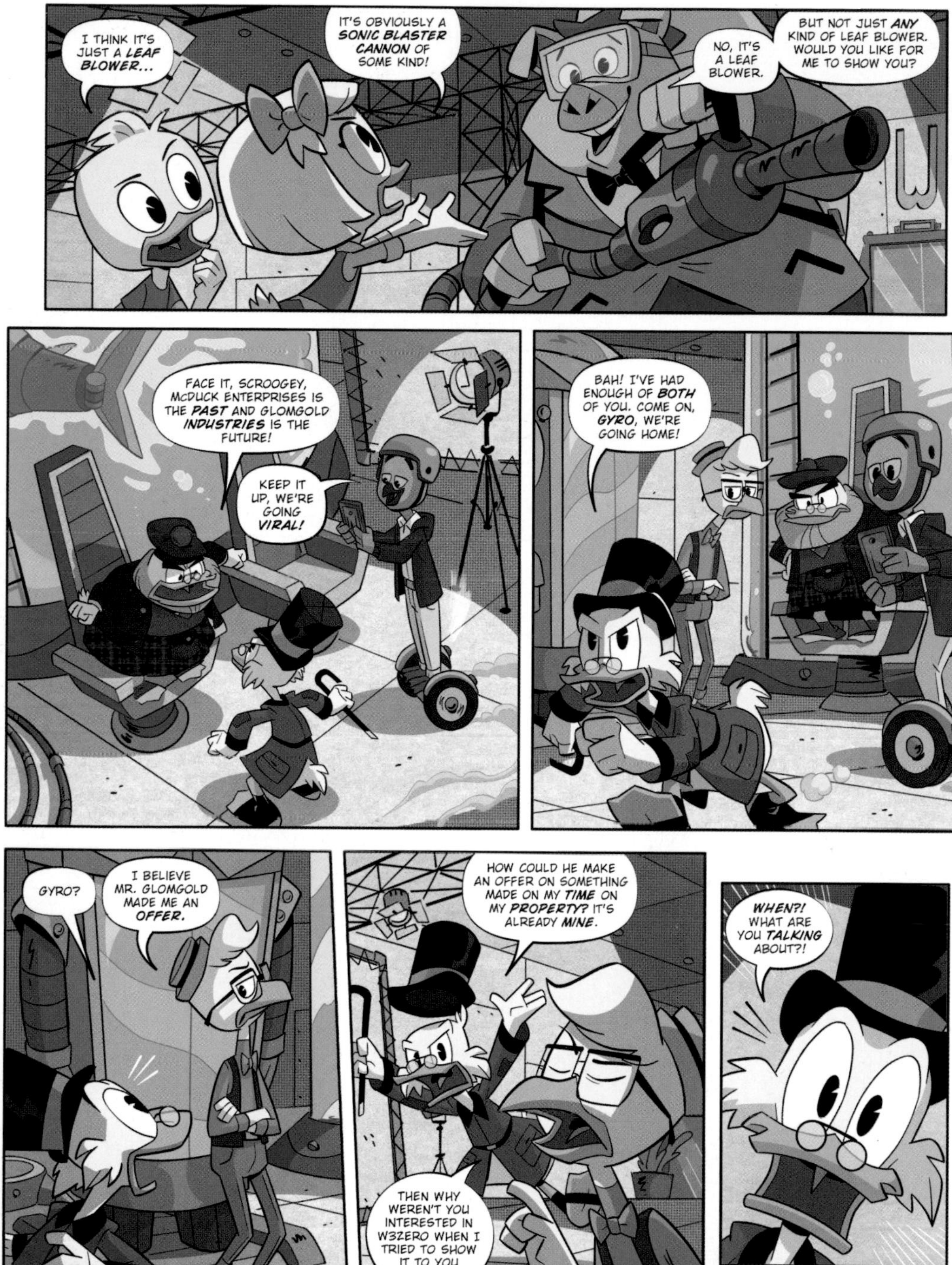
I THINK IT'S JUST A LEAF BLOWER...
IT'S OBVIOUSLY A SONIC BLASTER CANNON OF SOME KIND!
NO, IT'S A LEAF BLOWER.
BUT NOT JUST ANY KIND OF LEAF BLOWER. WOULD YOU LIKE FOR ME TO SHOW YOU?
FACE IT, SCROOGEY, McDUCK ENTERPRISES IS THE PAST AND GLOMGOLD INDUSTRIES IS THE FUTURE!
KEEP IT UP, WE'RE GOING VIRAL!
BAH! I'VE HAD ENOUGH OF BOTH OF YOU. COME ON, GYRO, WE'RE GOING HOME!
GYRO?
I BELIEVE MR. GLOMGOLD MADE ME AN OFFER.
HOW COULD HE MAKE AN OFFER ON SOMETHING MADE ON MY TIME ON MY PROPERTY? IT'S ALREADY MINE.
THEN WHY WEREN'T YOU INTERESTED IN W3ZERO WHEN I TRIED TO SHOW IT TO YOU BEFORE?
WHEN?! WHAT ARE YOU TALKING ABOUT?!

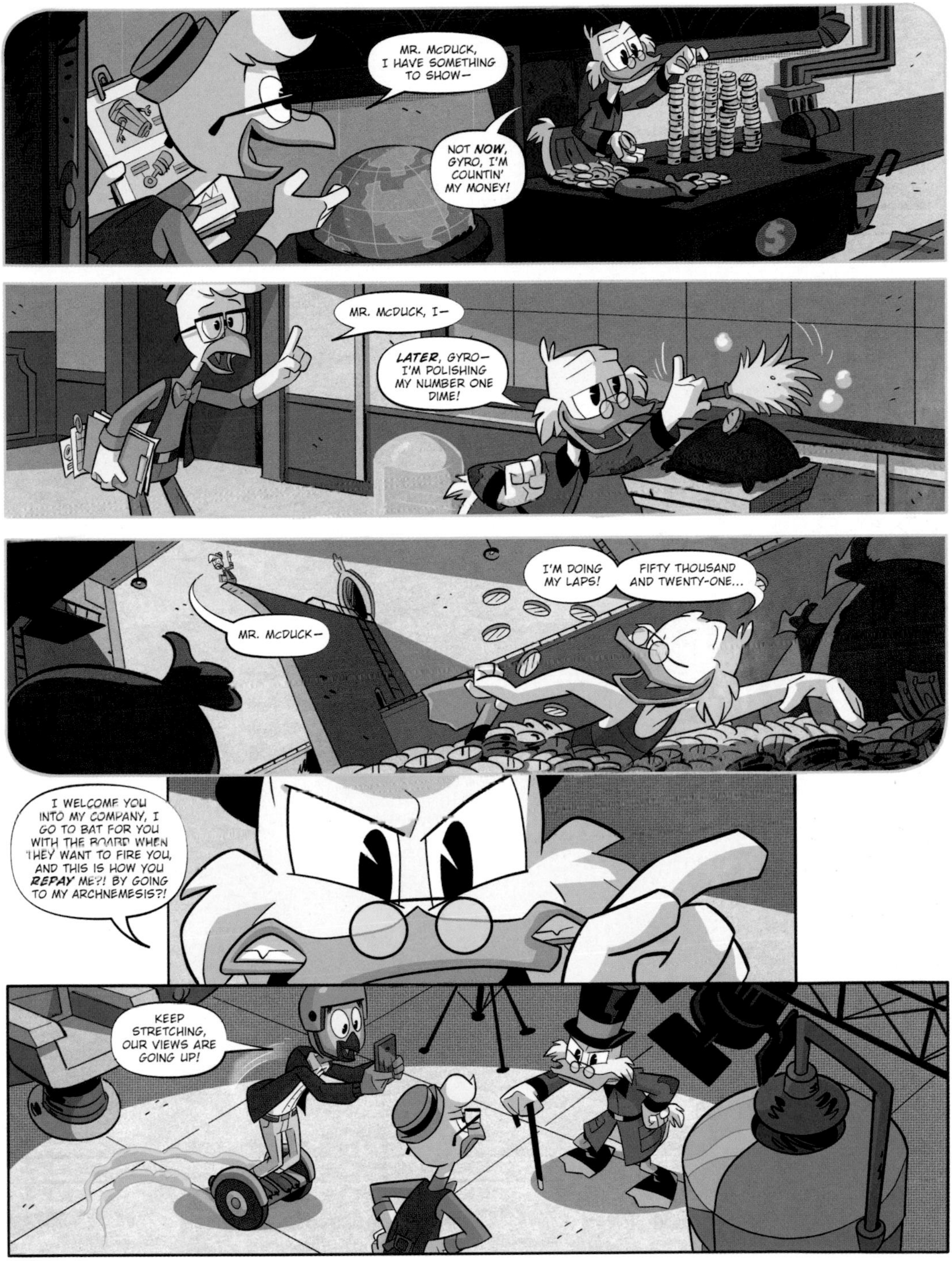
MR. McDUCK, I HAVE SOMETHING TO SHOW—
NOT NOW, GYRO, I'M COUNTIN' MY MONEY!
MR. McDUCK, I—
LATER, GYRO—I'M POLISHING MY NUMBER ONE DIME!
MR. McDUCK—
I'M DOING MY LAPS!
FIFTY THOUSAND AND TWENTY-ONE...
I WELCOME YOU INTO MY COMPANY, I GO TO BAT FOR YOU WITH THE BOARD WHEN THEY WANT TO FIRE YOU, AND THIS IS HOW YOU REPAY ME?! BY GOING TO MY ARCHNEMESIS?!
KEEP STRETCHING, OUR VIEWS ARE GOING UP!

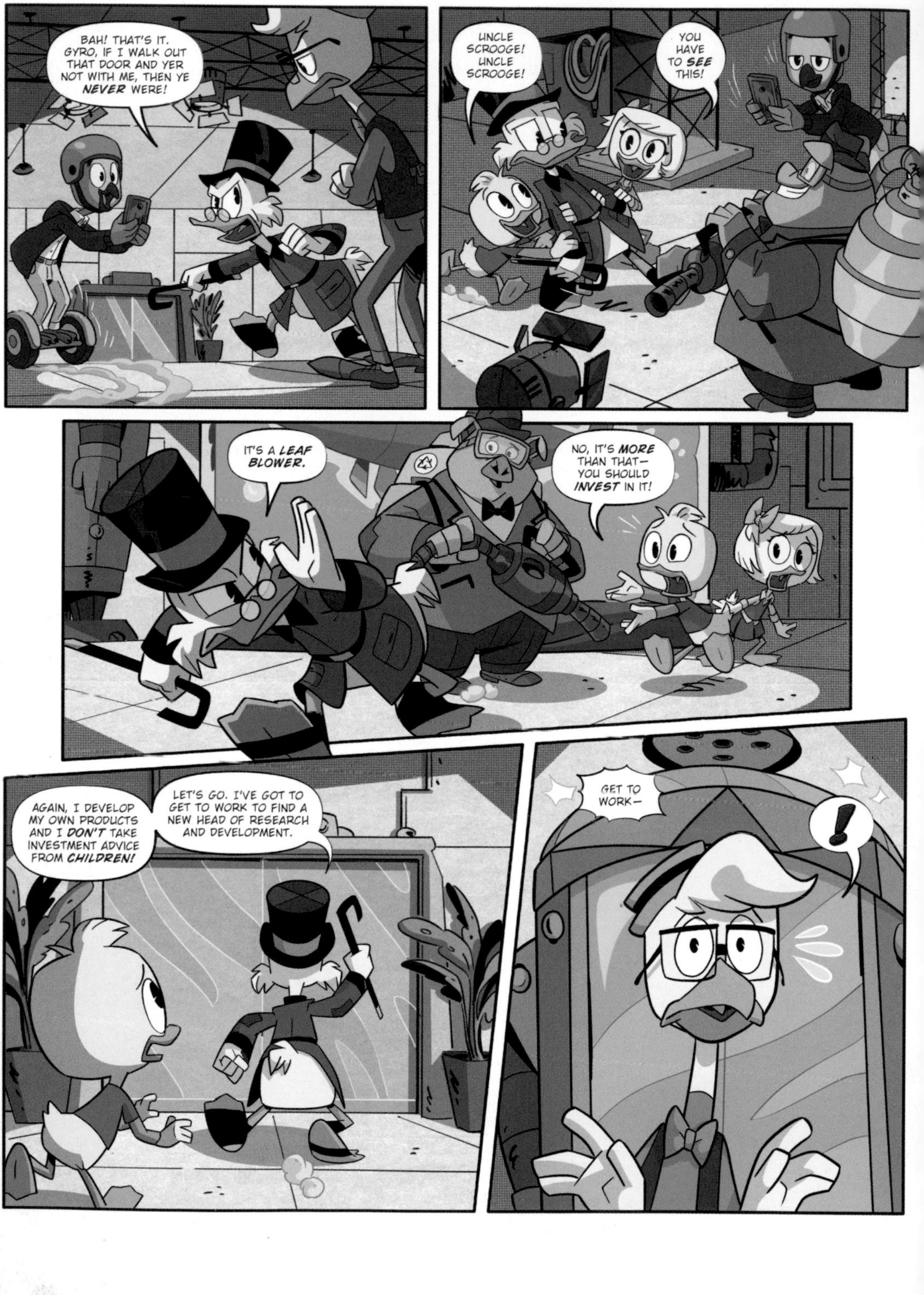
BAH! THAT'S IT. GYRO, IF I WALK OUT THAT DOOR AND YER NOT WITH ME, THEN YE *NEVER* WERE!
UNCLE SCROOGE! UNCLE SCROOGE!
YOU HAVE TO *SEE* THIS!
IT'S A *LEAF BLOWER.*
NO, IT'S *MORE* THAN THAT— YOU SHOULD *INVEST* IN IT!
AGAIN, I DEVELOP MY OWN PRODUCTS AND I *DON'T* TAKE INVESTMENT ADVICE FROM *CHILDREN!*
LET'S GO. I'VE GOT TO GET TO WORK TO FIND A NEW HEAD OF RESEARCH AND DEVELOPMENT.
GET TO WORK—
!

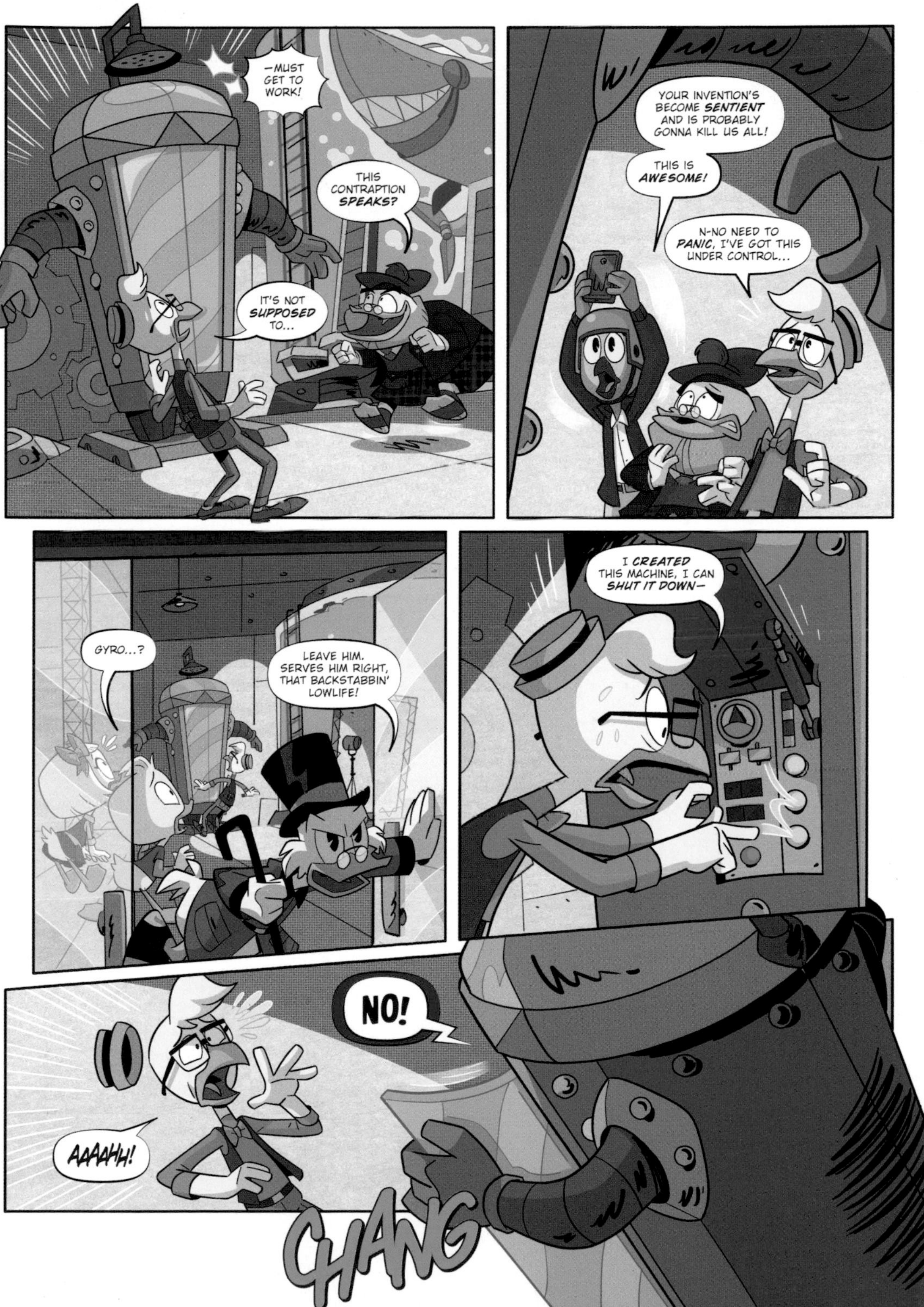
—MUST GET TO WORK!
THIS CONTRAPTION SPEAKS?
IT'S NOT SUPPOSED TO...
YOUR INVENTION'S BECOME SENTIENT AND IS PROBABLY GONNA KILL US ALL!
THIS IS AWESOME!
N-NO NEED TO PANIC, I'VE GOT THIS UNDER CONTROL...
GYRO...?
LEAVE HIM. SERVES HIM RIGHT, THAT BACKSTABBIN' LOWLIFE!
I CREATED THIS MACHINE, I CAN SHUT IT DOWN—
NO!
AAAAHH!
CHANG

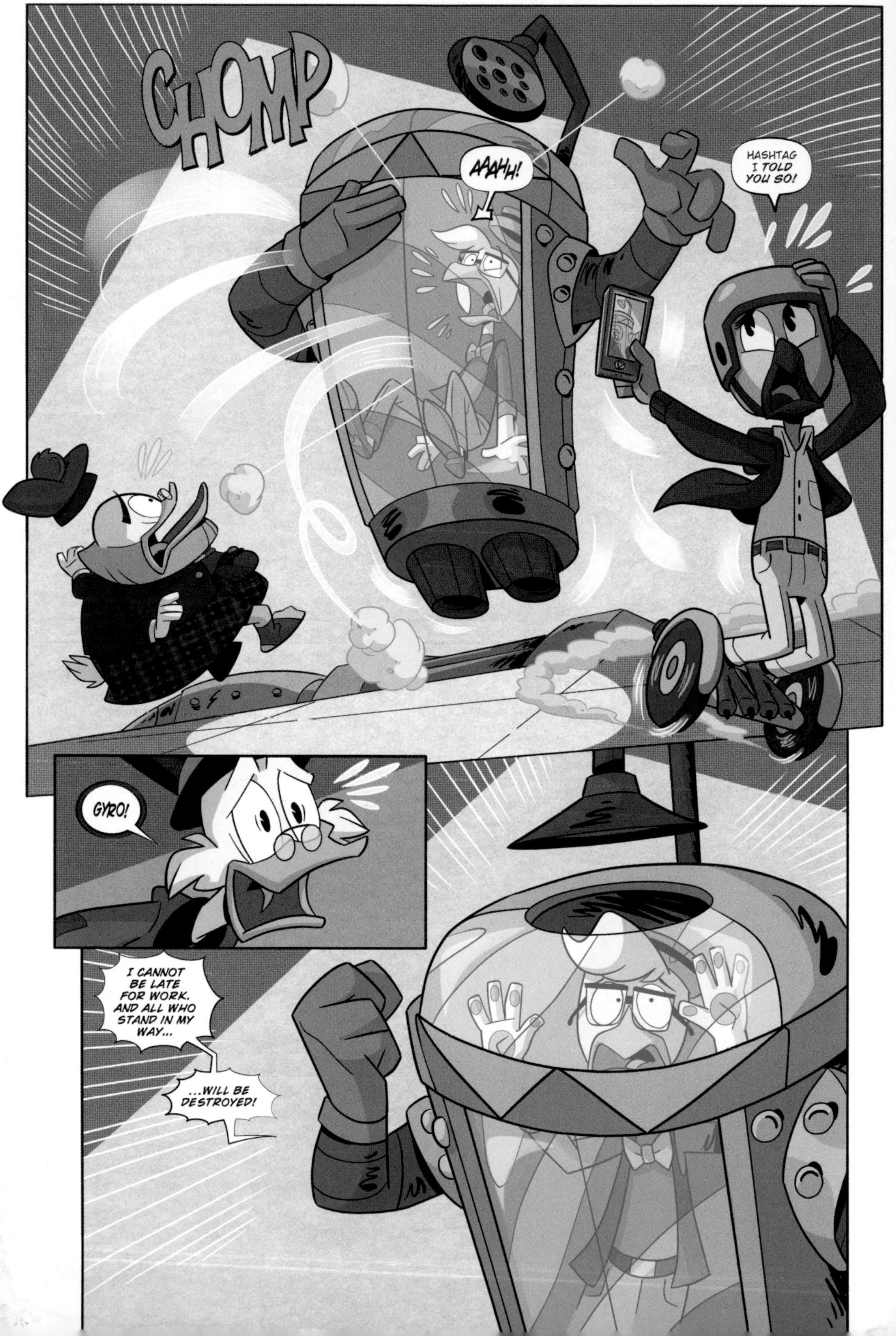
CHOMP
AAAHH!
HASHTAG I TOLD YOU SO!
GYRO!
I CANNOT BE LATE FOR WORK. AND ALL WHO STAND IN MY WAY...
...WILL BE DESTROYED!

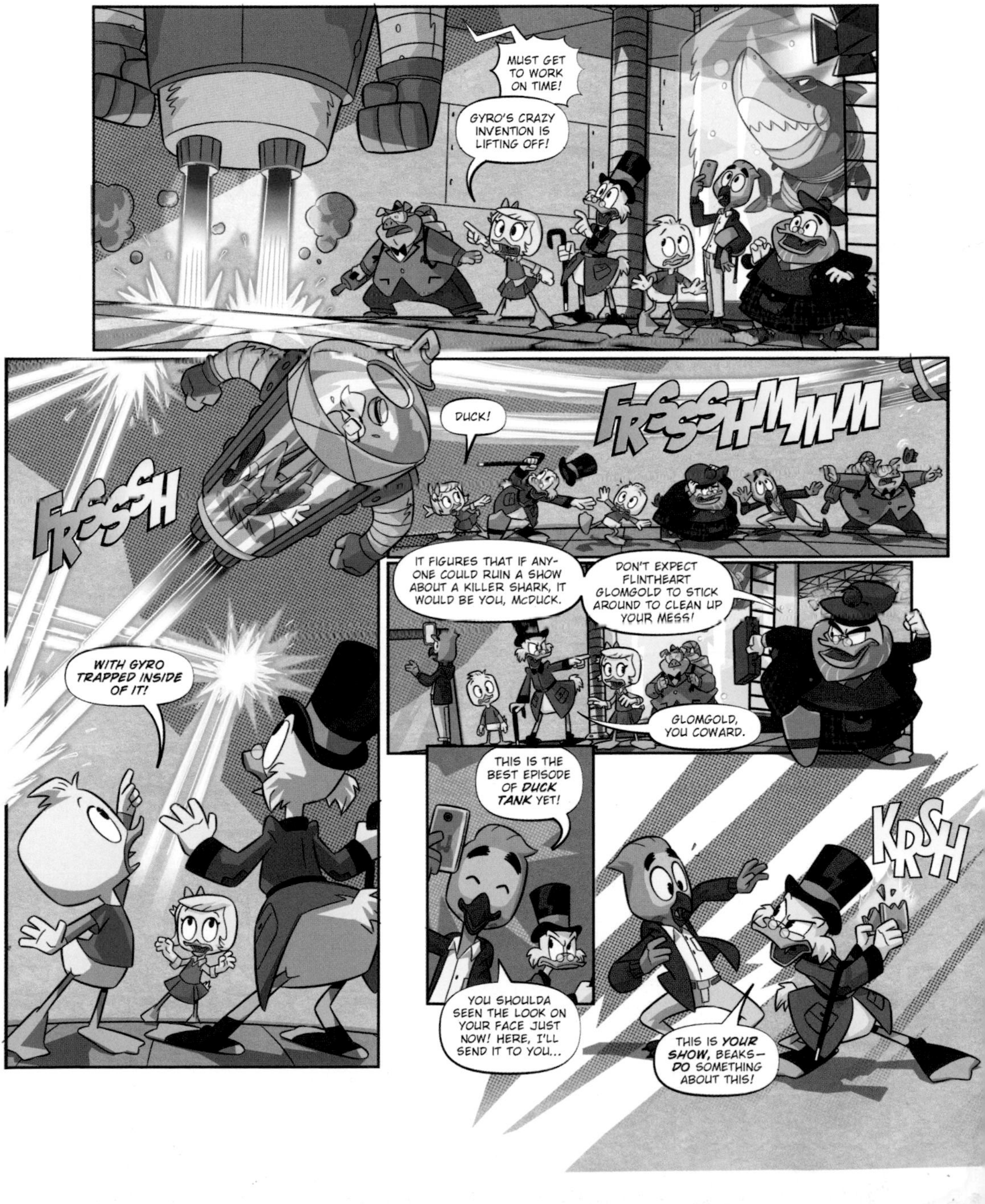
MUST GET TO WORK ON TIME!
GYRO'S CRAZY INVENTION IS LIFTING OFF!
DUCK!
FRSSSHMMMM
FRSSSH
WITH GYRO TRAPPED INSIDE OF IT!
IT FIGURES THAT IF ANY-ONE COULD RUIN A SHOW ABOUT A KILLER SHARK, IT WOULD BE YOU, McDUCK.
DON'T EXPECT FLINTHEART GLOMGOLD TO STICK AROUND TO CLEAN UP YOUR MESS!
GLOMGOLD, YOU COWARD.
THIS IS THE BEST EPISODE OF DUCK TANK YET!
YOU SHOULDA SEEN THE LOOK ON YOUR FACE JUST NOW! HERE, I'LL SEND IT TO YOU...
KRSH
THIS IS YOUR SHOW, BEAKS—DO SOMETHING ABOUT THIS!

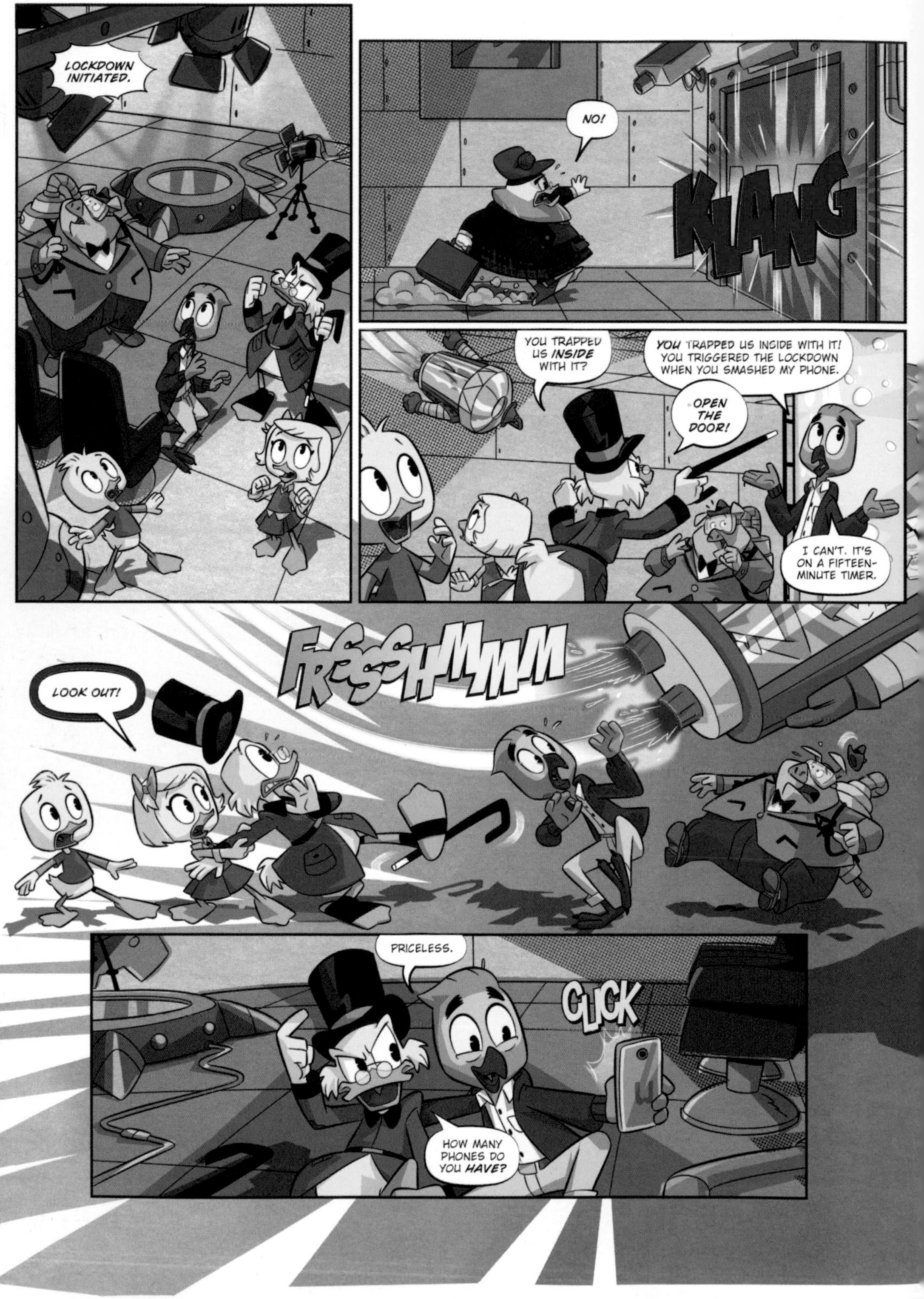
LOCKDOWN INITIATED.
NO!
KLANG
YOU TRAPPED US INSIDE WITH IT?
YOU TRAPPED US INSIDE WITH IT! YOU TRIGGERED THE LOCKDOWN WHEN YOU SMASHED MY PHONE.
OPEN THE DOOR!
I CAN'T. IT'S ON A FIFTEEN-MINUTE TIMER.
FRESSHMMMM
LOOK OUT!
PRICELESS.
CLICK
HOW MANY PHONES DO YOU HAVE?

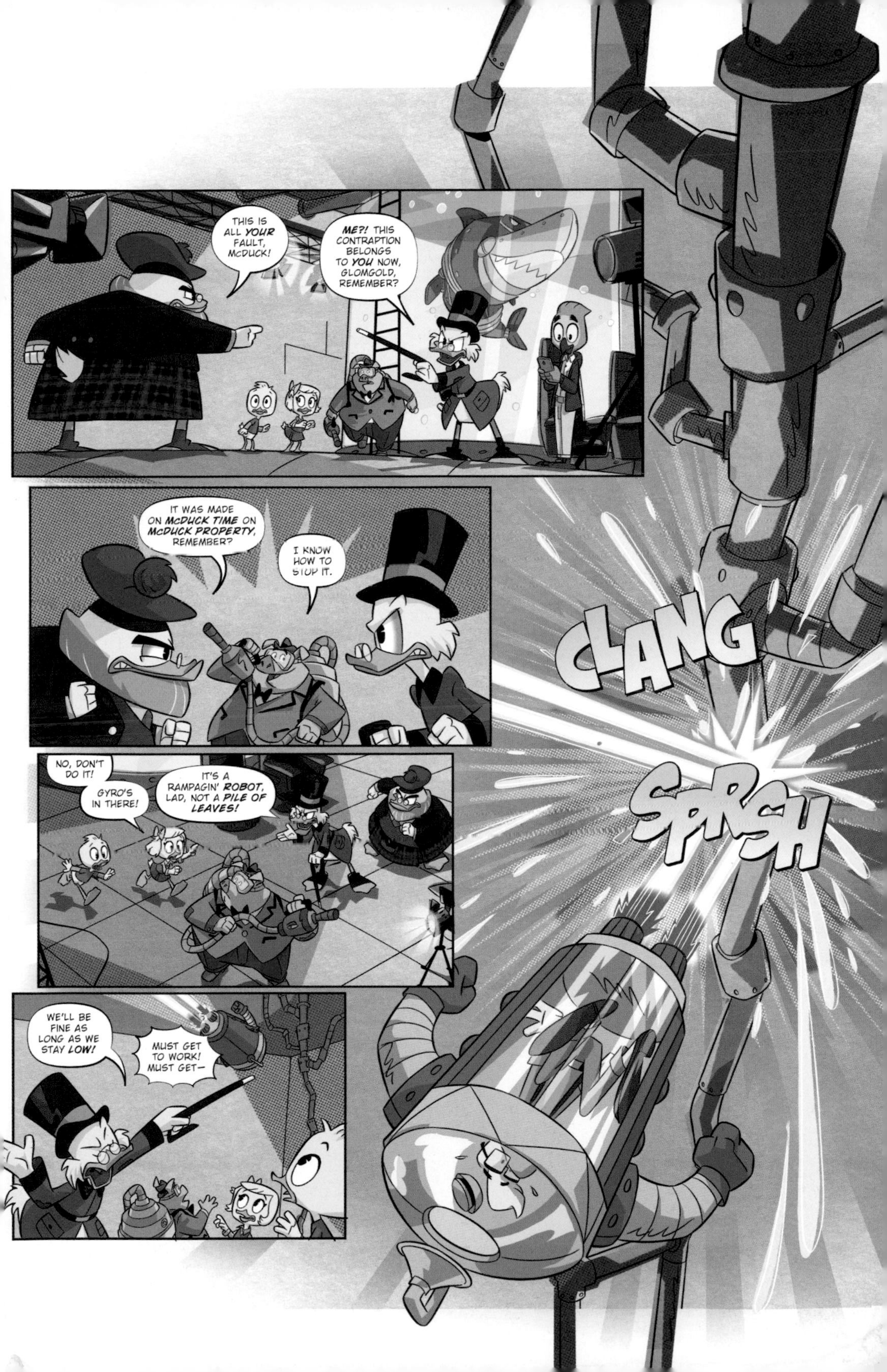
THIS IS ALL YOUR FAULT, McDUCK!
ME?! THIS CONTRAPTION BELONGS TO YOU NOW, GLOMGOLD, REMEMBER?
IT WAS MADE ON McDUCK TIME ON McDUCK PROPERTY, REMEMBER?
I KNOW HOW TO STOP IT.
NO, DON'T DO IT!
GYRO'S IN THERE!
IT'S A RAMPAGIN' ROBOT, LAD, NOT A PILE OF LEAVES!
WE'LL BE FINE AS LONG AS WE STAY LOW!
MUST GET TO WORK! MUST GET—
CLANG
SPRSH

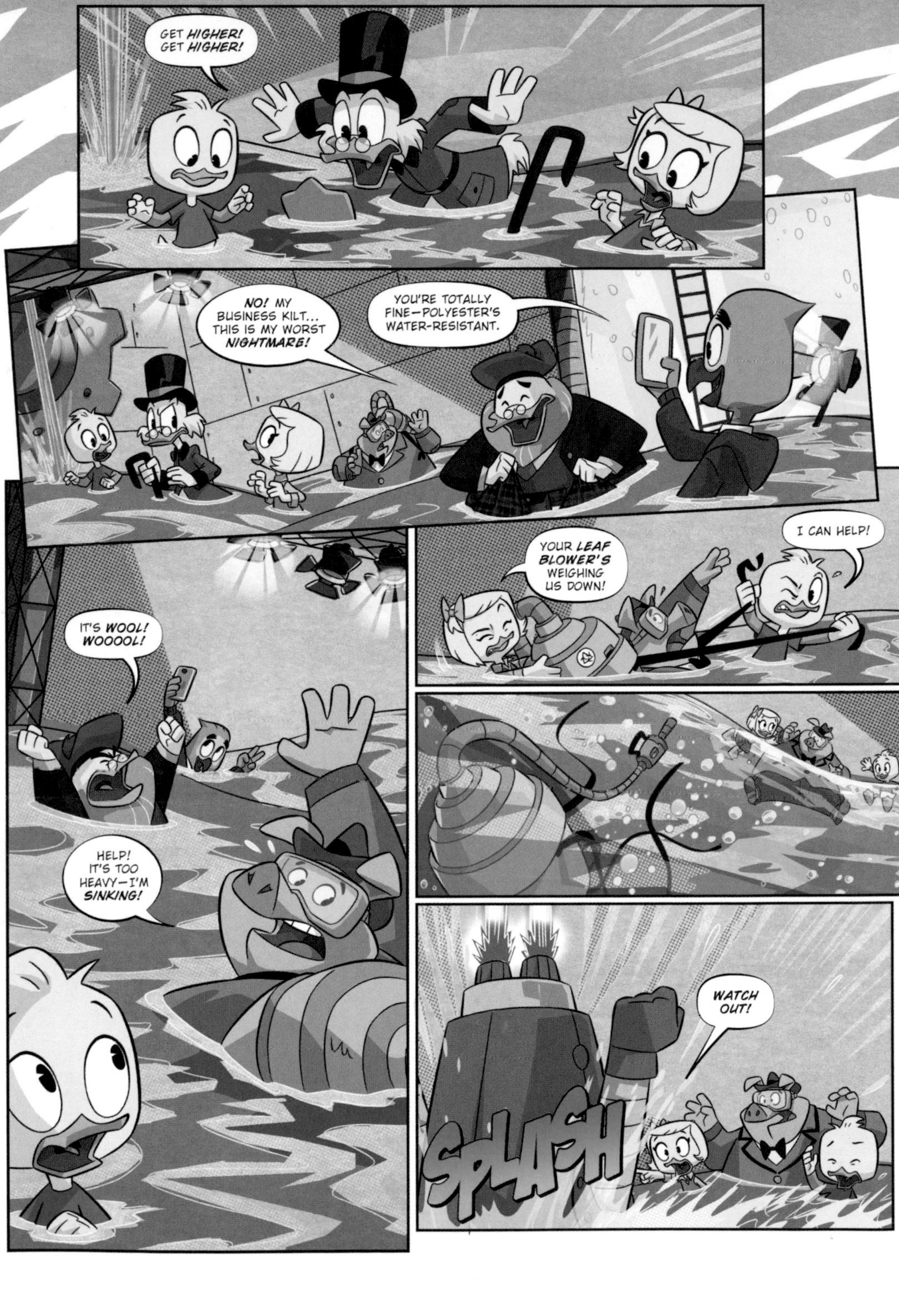
GET HIGHER! GET HIGHER!
NO! MY BUSINESS KILT... THIS IS MY WORST NIGHTMARE!
YOU'RE TOTALLY FINE—POLYESTER'S WATER-RESISTANT.
IT'S WOOL! WOOOOL!
HELP! IT'S TOO HEAVY—I'M SINKING!
YOUR LEAF BLOWER'S WEIGHING US DOWN!
I CAN HELP!
WATCH OUT!
SPLASH

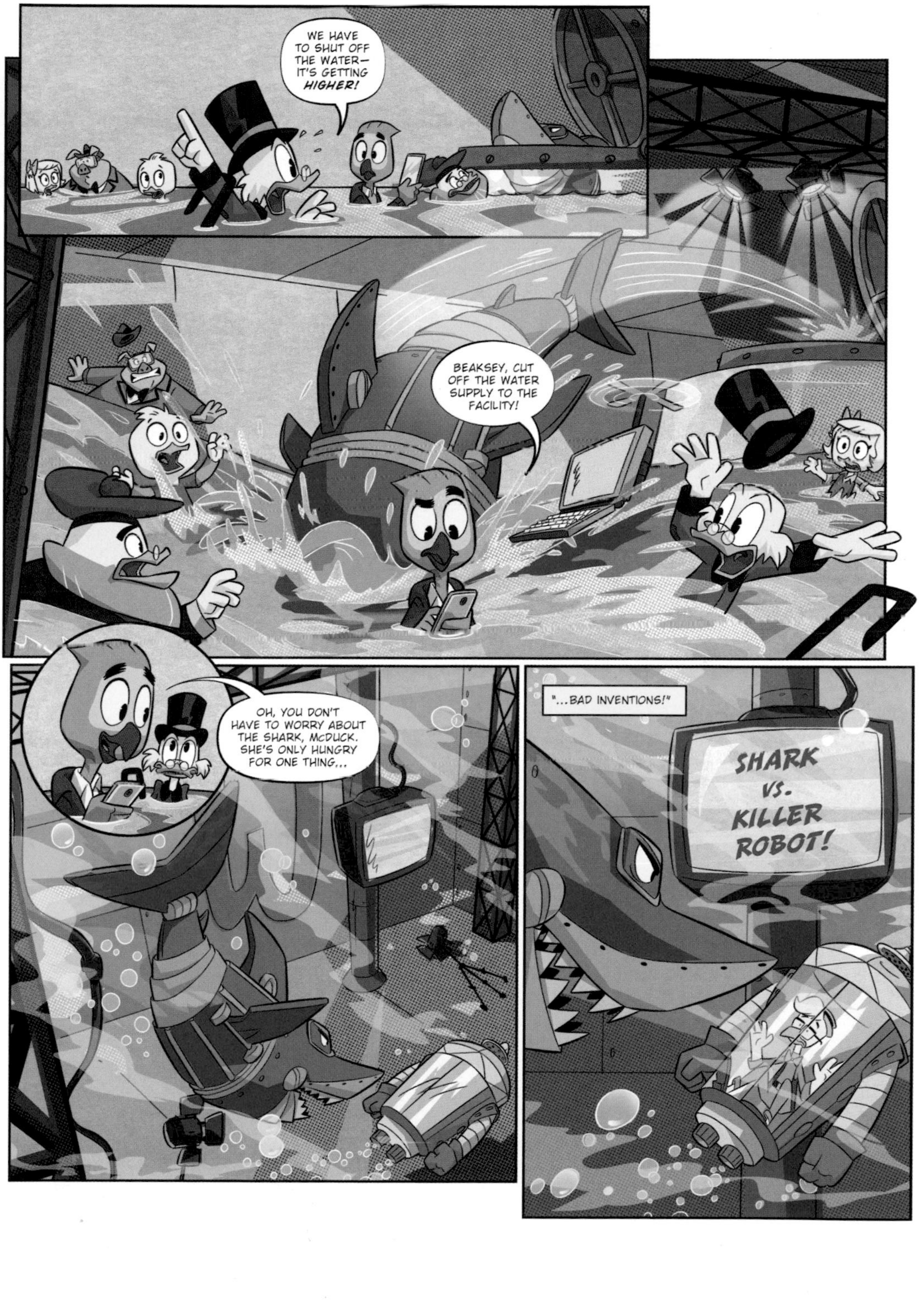
WE HAVE TO SHUT OFF THE WATER— IT'S GETTING HIGHER!
BEAKSEY, CUT OFF THE WATER SUPPLY TO THE FACILITY!
OH, YOU DON'T HAVE TO WORRY ABOUT THE SHARK, McDUCK. SHE'S ONLY HUNGRY FOR ONE THING...
"...BAD INVENTIONS!"
SHARK VS. KILLER ROBOT!

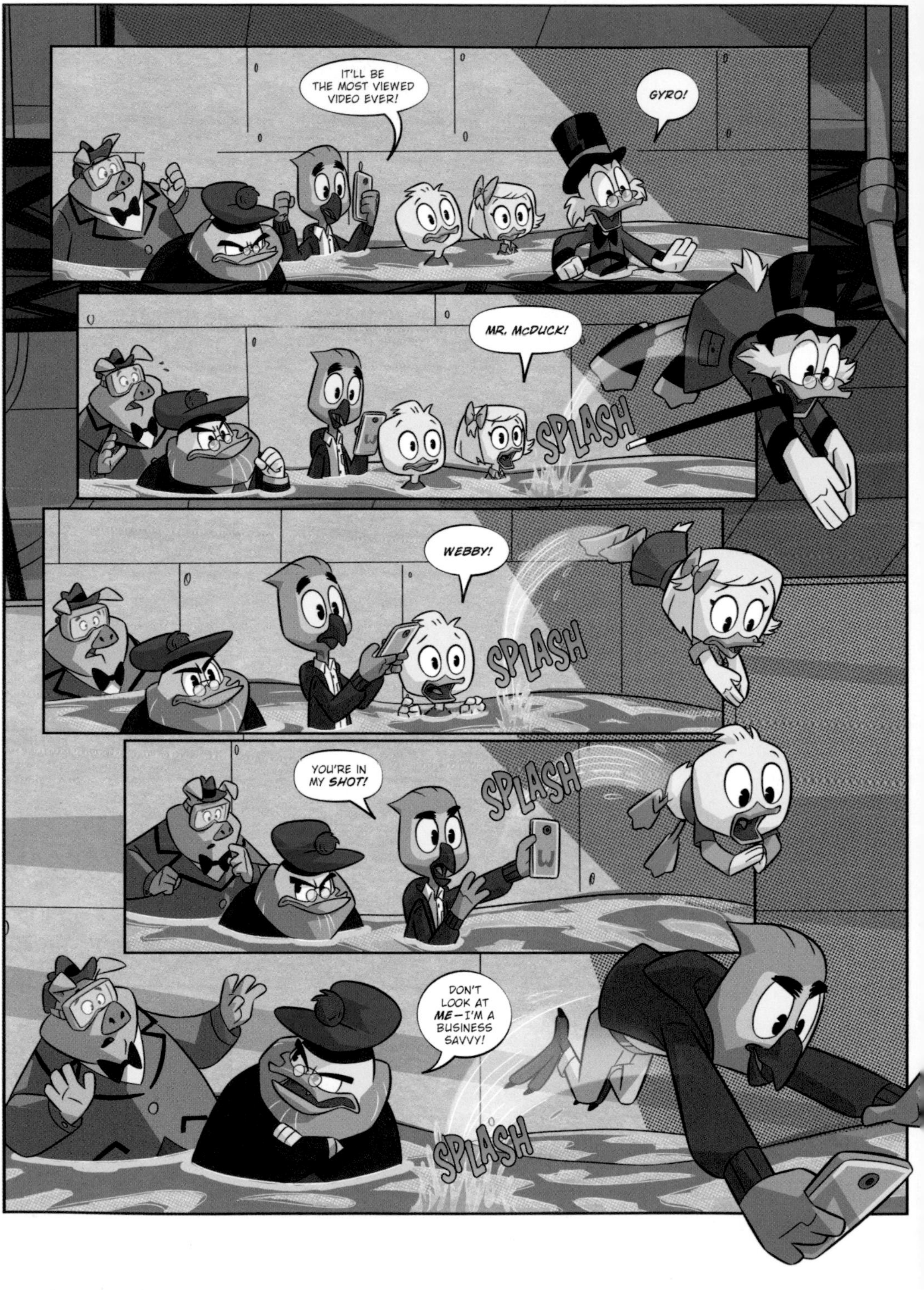
IT'LL BE THE MOST VIEWED VIDEO EVER!
GYRO!
MR. McDUCK!
SPLASH
WEBBY!
SPLASH
YOU'RE IN MY SHOT!
SPLASH
DON'T LOOK AT ME—I'M A BUSINESS SAVVY!
SPLASH

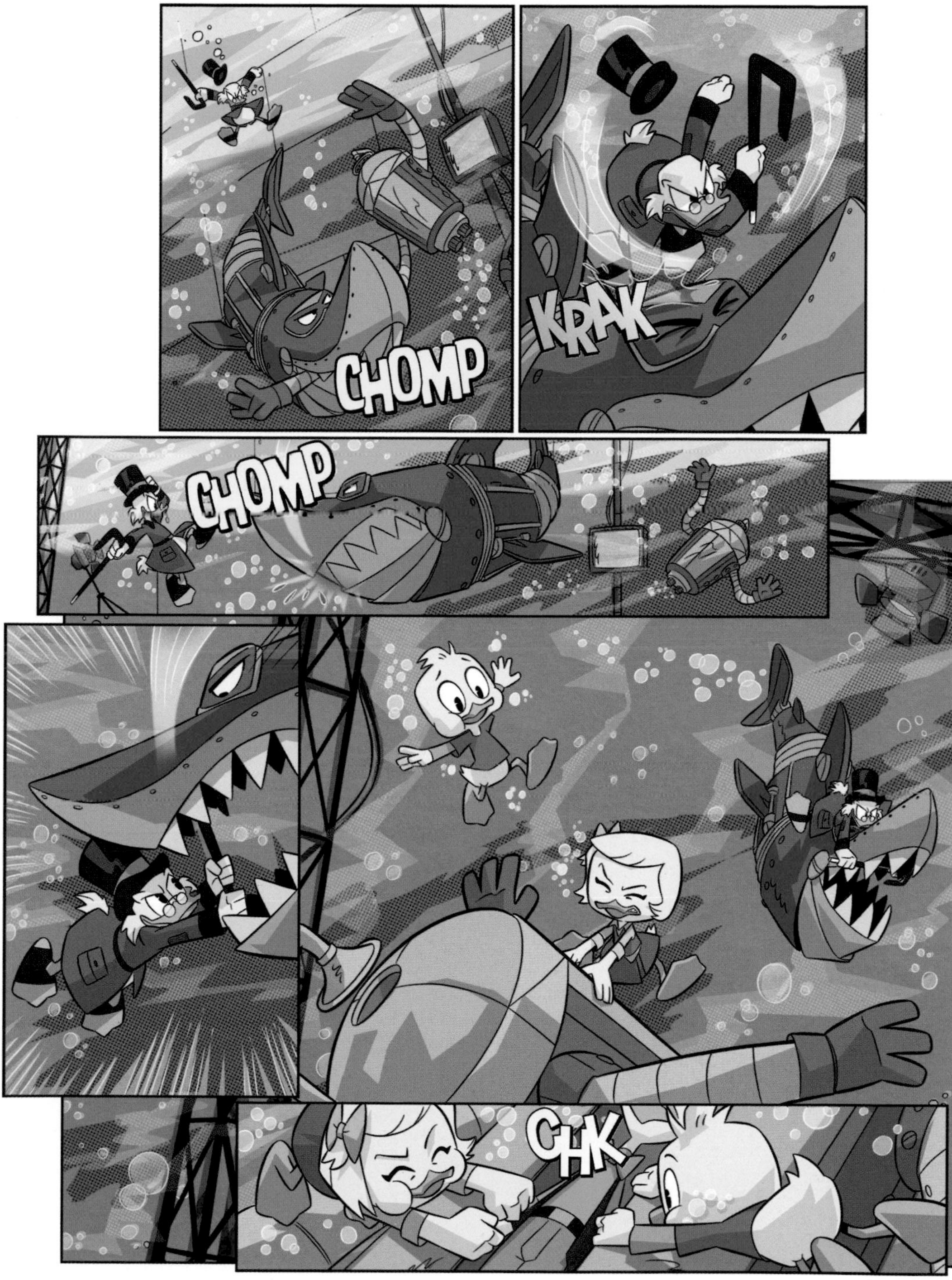
CHOMP
KRAK
CHOMP
CHK

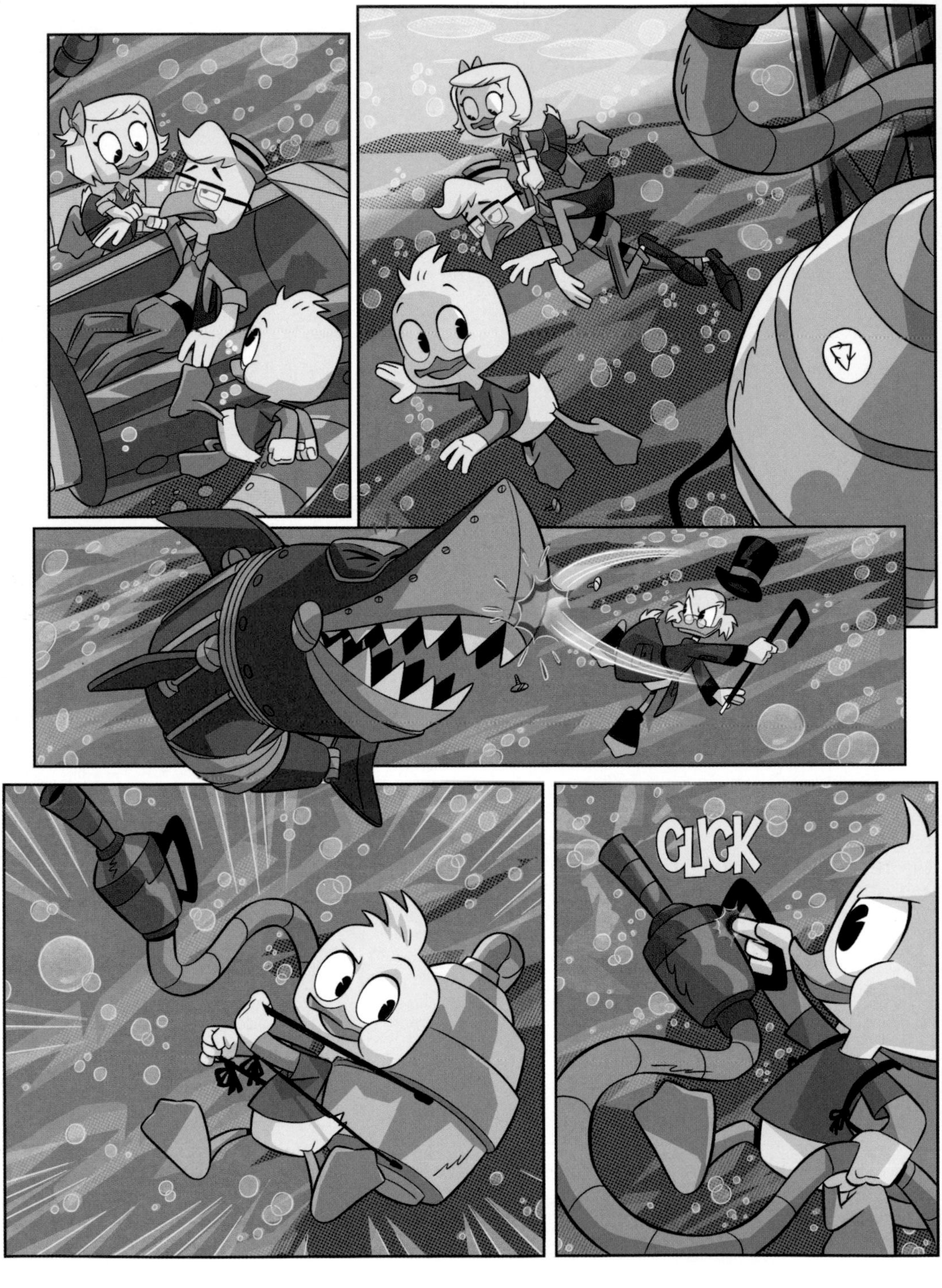
CLICK

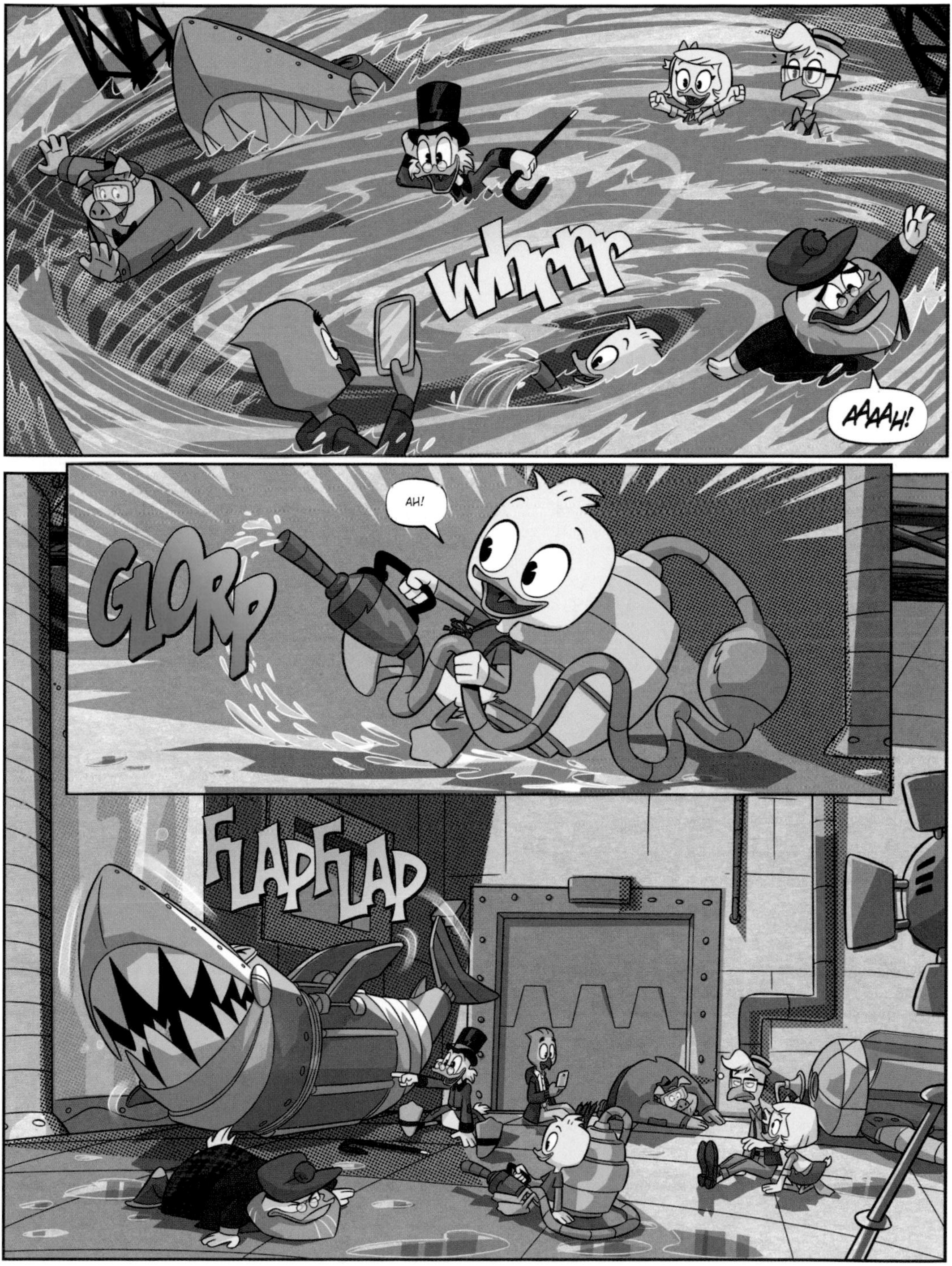
WHRRR
AAAAH!
GLORP
AH!
FLAPFLAP

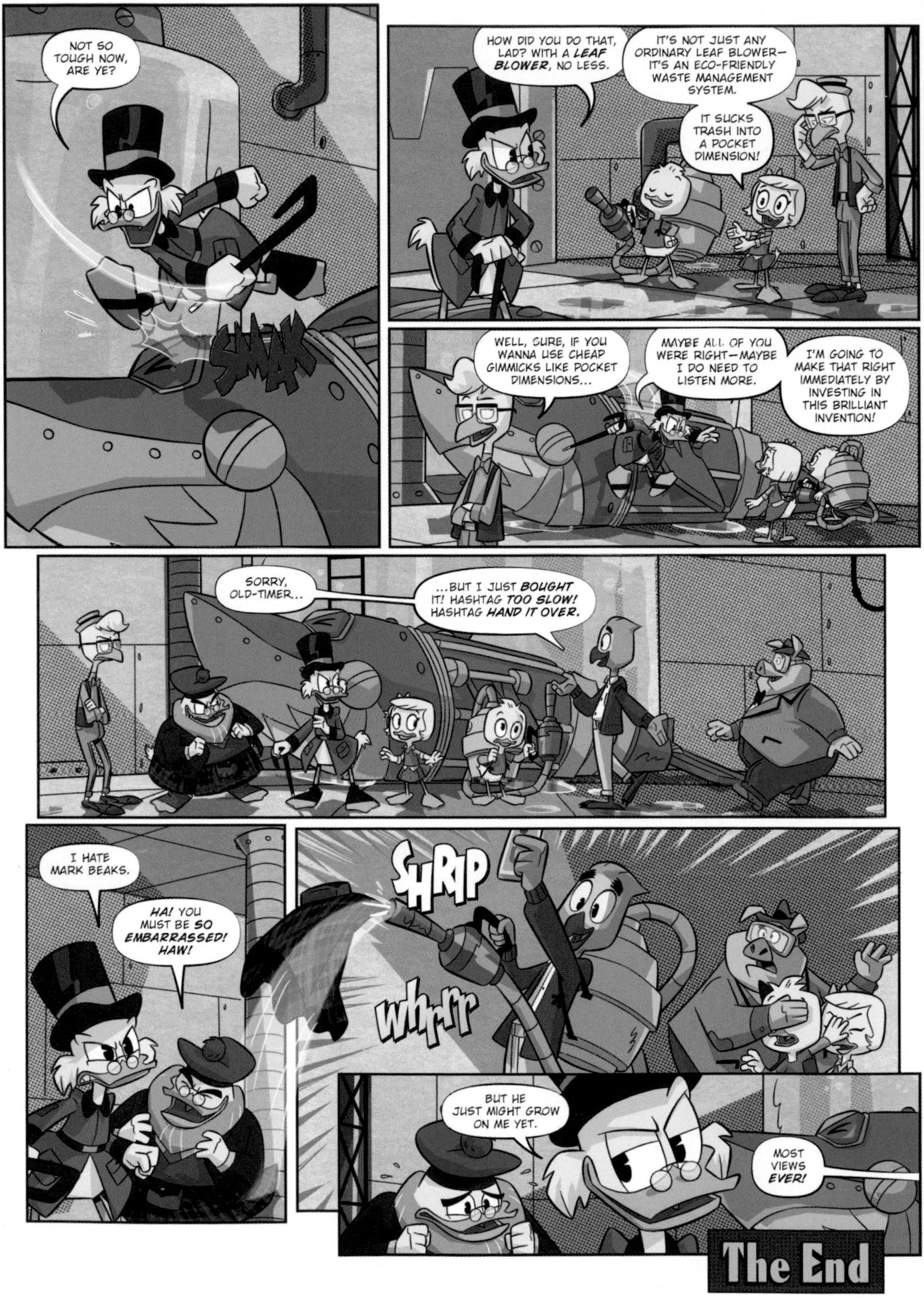
NOT SO TOUGH NOW, ARE YE?
SMAK
HOW DID YOU DO THAT, LAD? WITH A LEAF BLOWER, NO LESS.
IT'S NOT JUST ANY ORDINARY LEAF BLOWER—IT'S AN ECO-FRIENDLY WASTE MANAGEMENT SYSTEM.
IT SUCKS TRASH INTO A POCKET DIMENSION!
WELL, SURE, IF YOU WANNA USE CHEAP GIMMICKS LIKE POCKET DIMENSIONS...
MAYBE ALL OF YOU WERE RIGHT—MAYBE I DO NEED TO LISTEN MORE.
I'M GOING TO MAKE THAT RIGHT IMMEDIATELY BY INVESTING IN THIS BRILLIANT INVENTION!
SORRY, OLD-TIMER...
...BUT I JUST BOUGHT IT! HASHTAG TOO SLOW! HASHTAG HAND IT OVER.
I HATE MARK BEAKS.
HA! YOU MUST BE SO EMBARRASSED! HAW!
SHRIP
whrrr
BUT HE JUST MIGHT GROW ON ME YET.
MOST VIEWS EVER!
The End

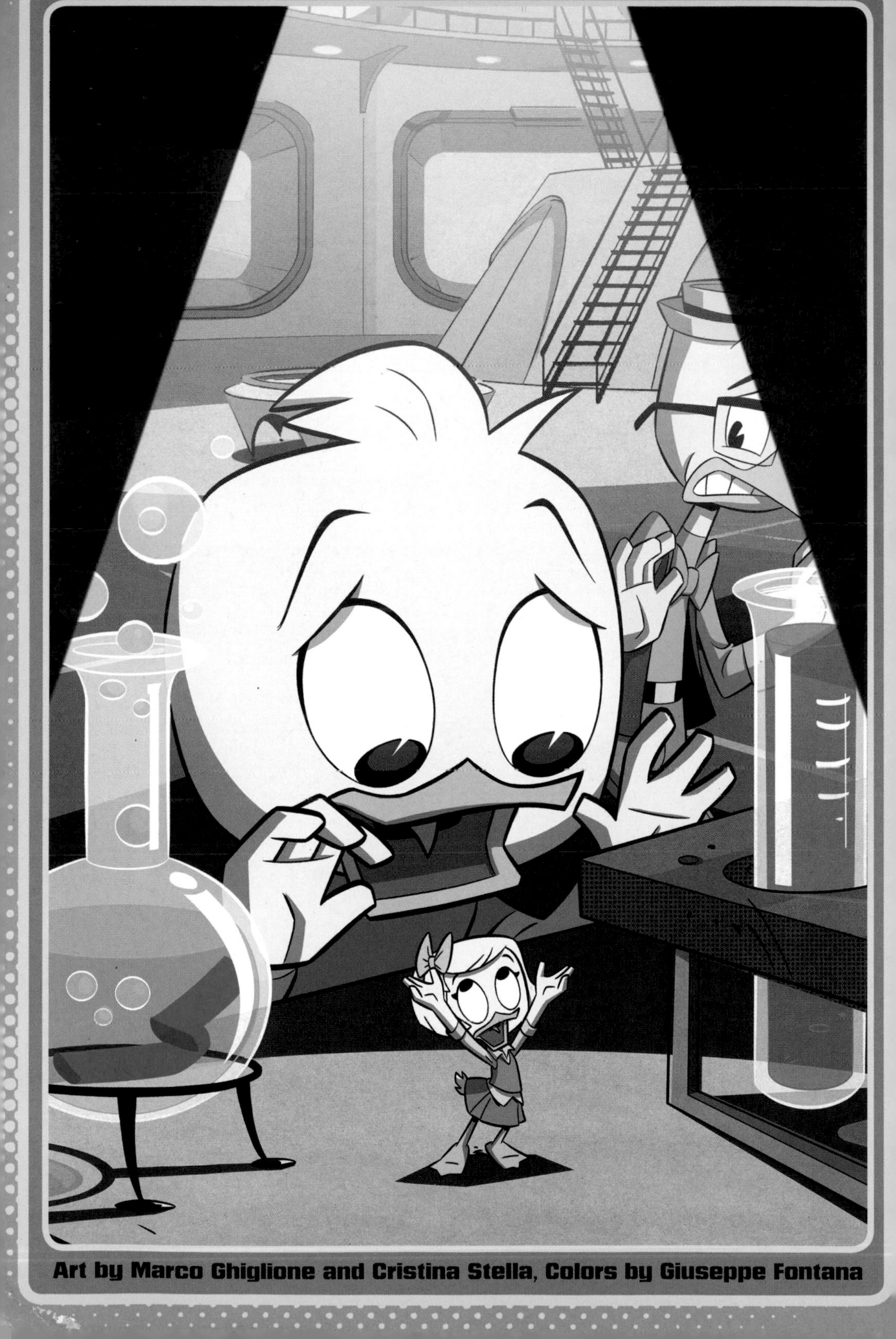

Art by Marco Ghiglione and Cristina Stella, Colors by Giuseppe Fontana

Disney

DuckTales

THE INCREDIBLE SHRINKING WEBBY!

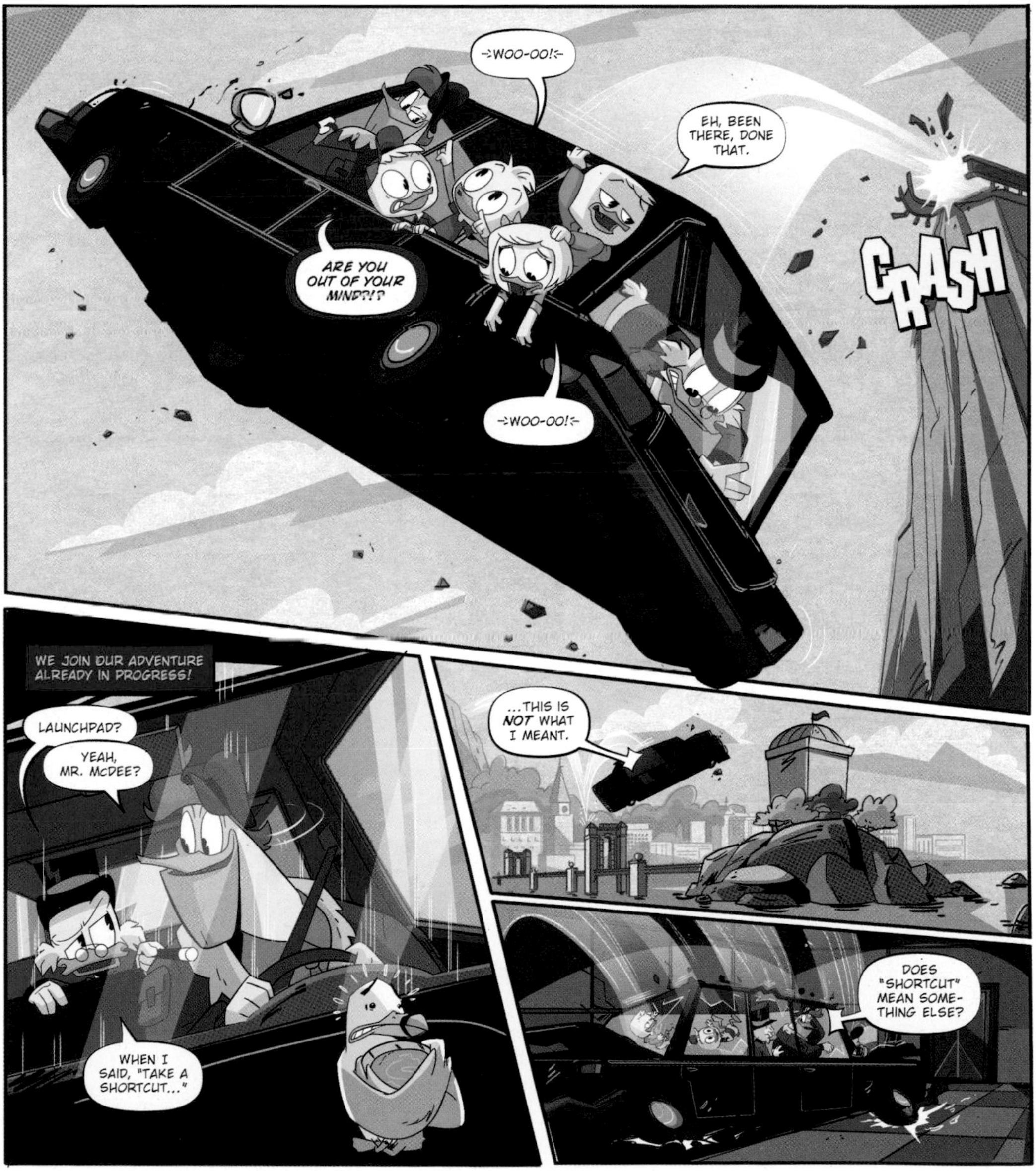
WOO-OO!
ARE YOU OUT OF YOUR MIND?!?
EH, BEEN THERE, DONE THAT.
WOO-OO!
CRASH
WE JOIN OUR ADVENTURE ALREADY IN PROGRESS!
LAUNCHPAD?
YEAH, MR. McDEE?
WHEN I SAID, "TAKE A SHORTCUT..."
...THIS IS NOT WHAT I MEANT.
DOES "SHORTCUT" MEAN SOME-THING ELSE?

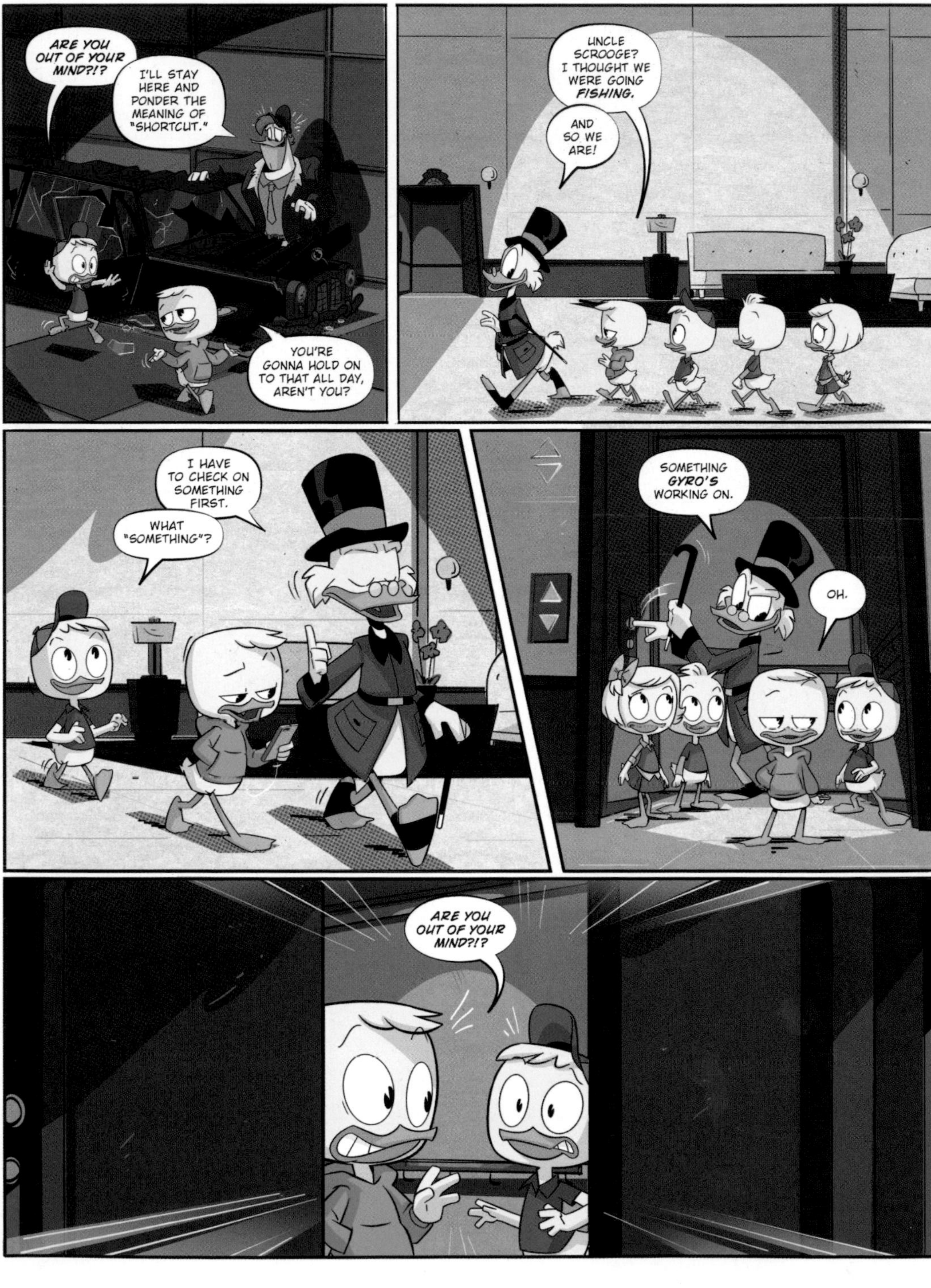
ARE YOU OUT OF YOUR MIND?!?
I'LL STAY HERE AND PONDER THE MEANING OF "SHORTCUT."
YOU'RE GONNA HOLD ON TO THAT ALL DAY, AREN'T YOU?
UNCLE SCROOGE? I THOUGHT WE WERE GOING FISHING.
AND SO WE ARE!
I HAVE TO CHECK ON SOMETHING FIRST.
WHAT "SOMETHING"?
SOMETHING GYRO'S WORKING ON.
OH.
ARE YOU OUT OF YOUR MIND?!?

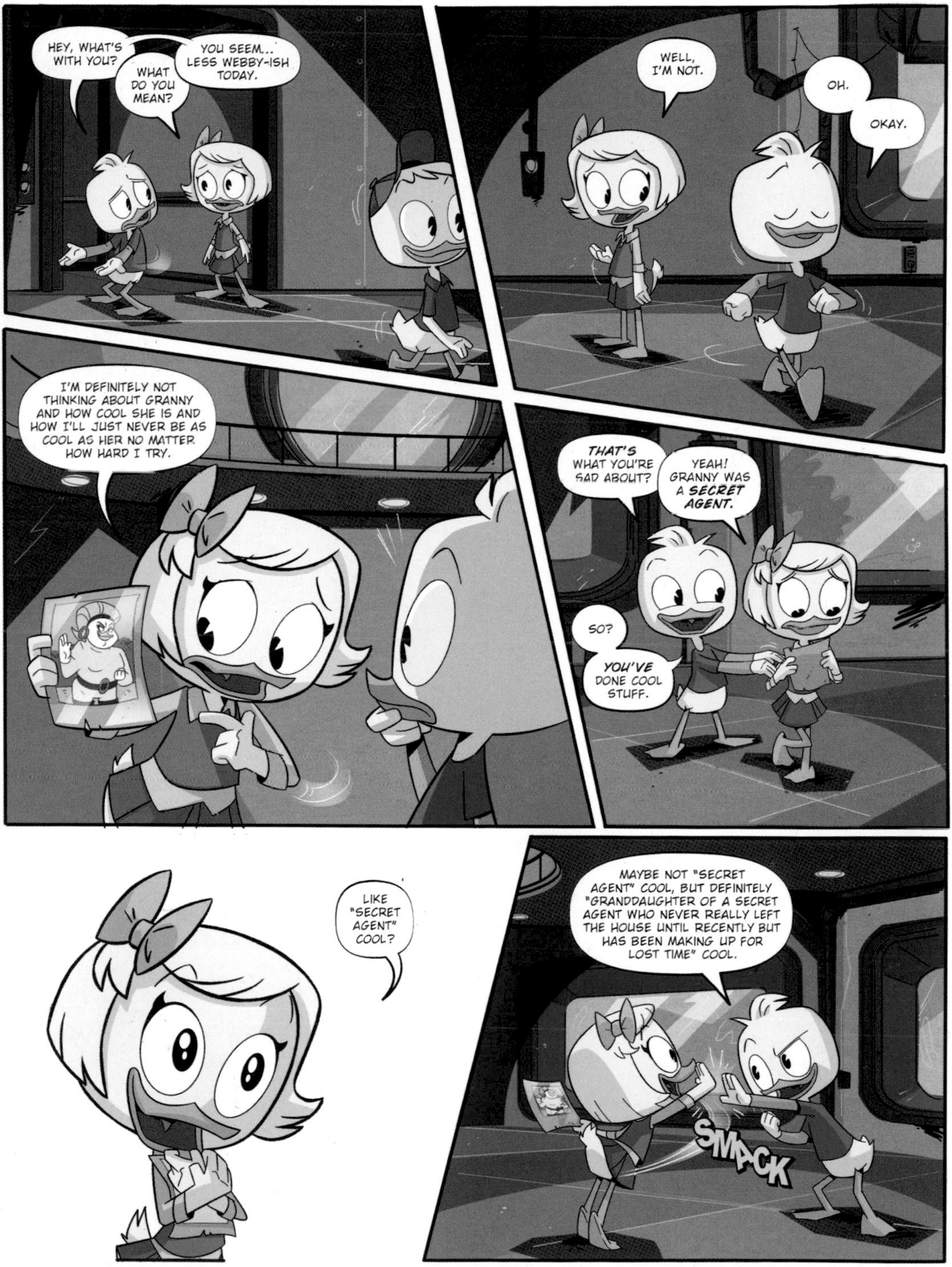
HEY, WHAT'S WITH YOU?
WHAT DO YOU MEAN?
YOU SEEM... LESS WEBBY-ISH TODAY.
WELL, I'M NOT.
OH.
OKAY.
I'M DEFINITELY NOT THINKING ABOUT GRANNY AND HOW COOL SHE IS AND HOW I'LL JUST NEVER BE AS COOL AS HER NO MATTER HOW HARD I TRY.
THAT'S WHAT YOU'RE SAD ABOUT?
YEAH! GRANNY WAS A SECRET AGENT.
SO?
YOU'VE DONE COOL STUFF.
LIKE "SECRET AGENT" COOL?
MAYBE NOT "SECRET AGENT" COOL, BUT DEFINITELY "GRANDDAUGHTER OF A SECRET AGENT WHO NEVER REALLY LEFT THE HOUSE UNTIL RECENTLY BUT HAS BEEN MAKING UP FOR LOST TIME" COOL.
SMACK

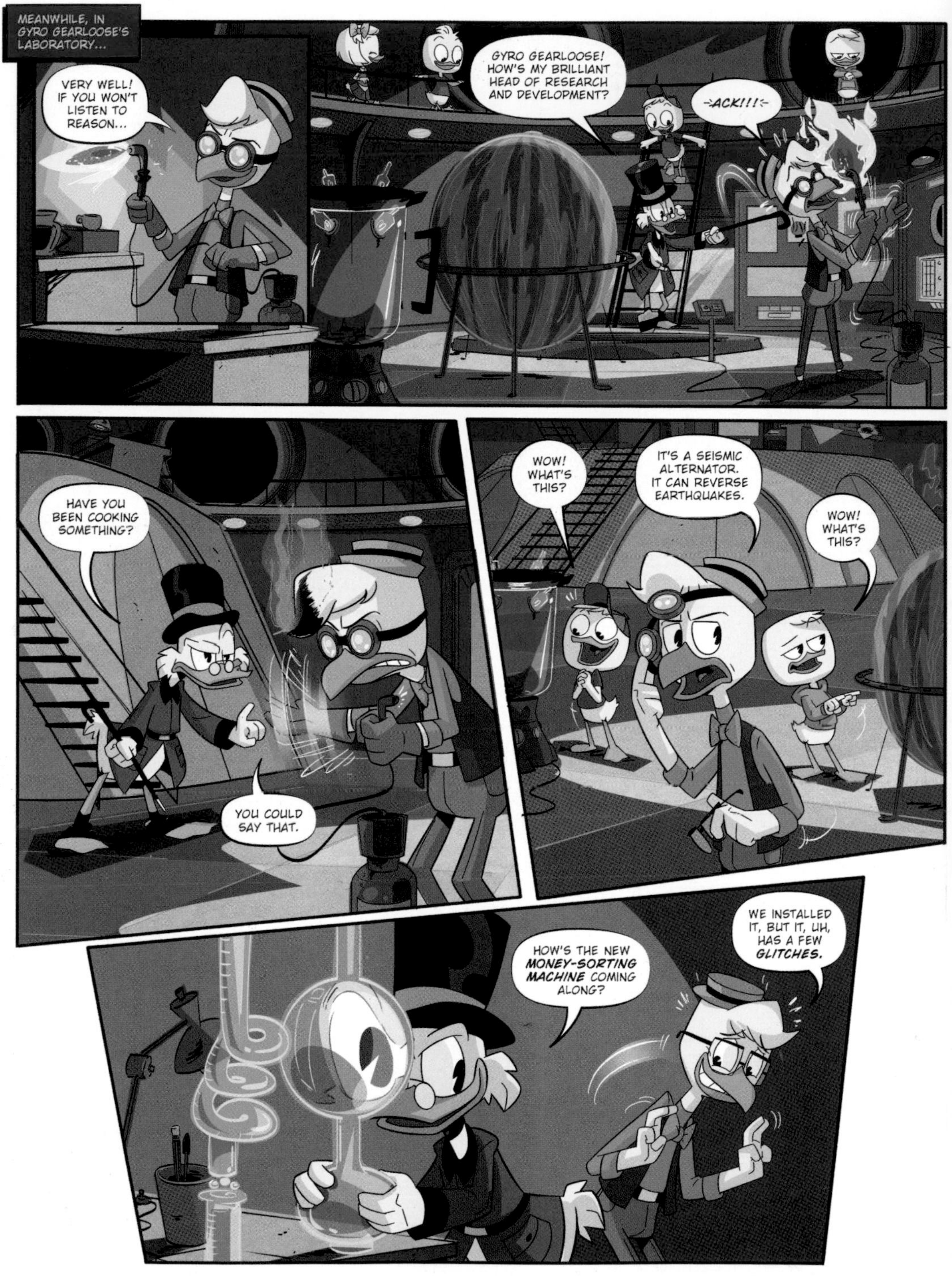
MEANWHILE, IN GYRO GEARLOOSE'S LABORATORY...
VERY WELL! IF YOU WON'T LISTEN TO REASON...
GYRO GEARLOOSE! HOW'S MY BRILLIANT HEAD OF RESEARCH AND DEVELOPMENT?
-ACK!!!-
HAVE YOU BEEN COOKING SOMETHING?
YOU COULD SAY THAT.
WOW! WHAT'S THIS?
IT'S A SEISMIC ALTERNATOR. IT CAN REVERSE EARTHQUAKES.
WOW! WHAT'S THIS?
HOW'S THE NEW **MONEY-SORTING MACHINE** COMING ALONG?
WE INSTALLED IT, BUT IT, UH, HAS A FEW ***GLITCHES.***

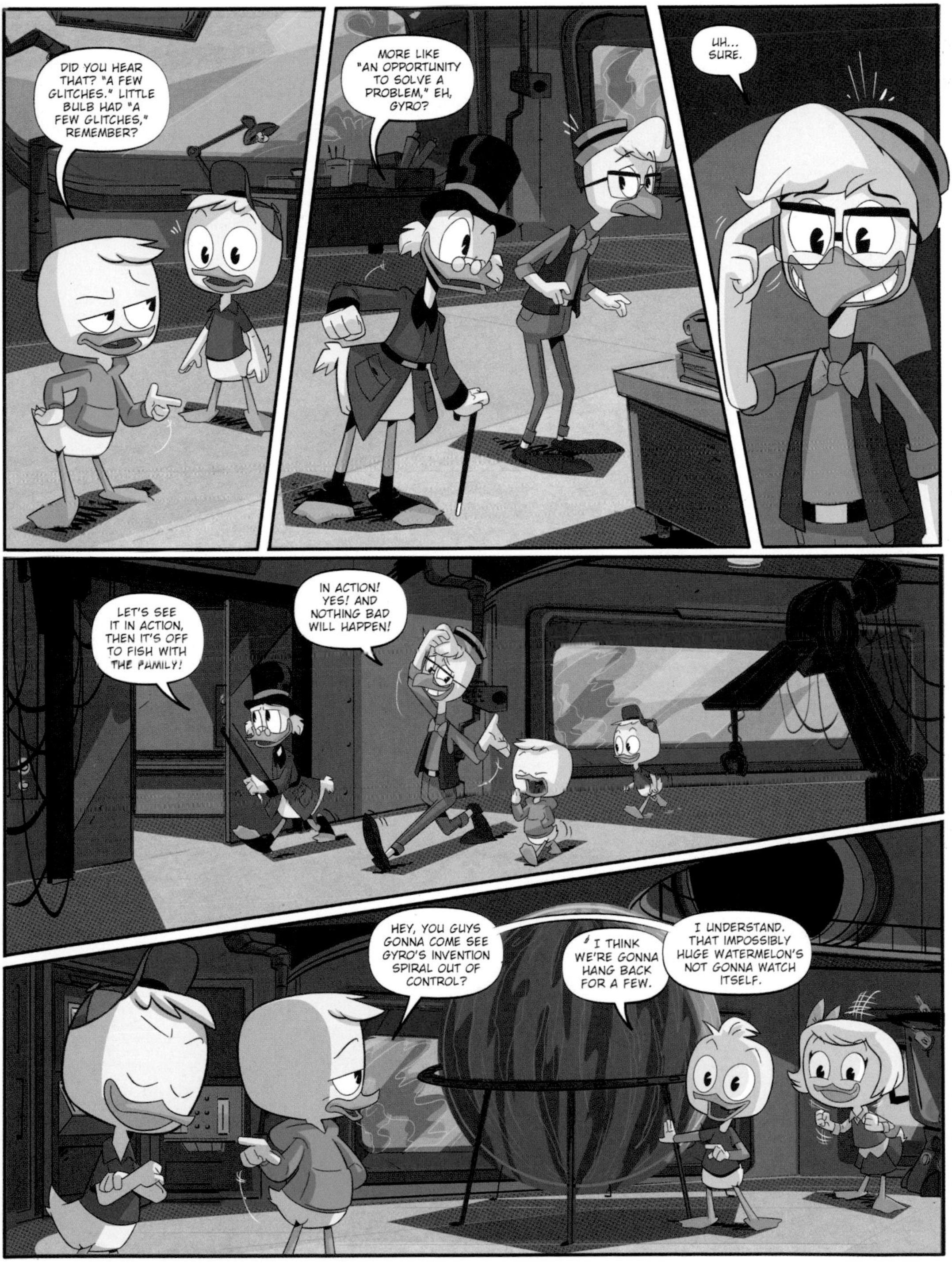
DID YOU HEAR THAT? "A FEW GLITCHES." LITTLE BULB HAD "A FEW GLITCHES," REMEMBER?
MORE LIKE "AN OPPORTUNITY TO SOLVE A PROBLEM," EH, GYRO?
UH... SURE.
LET'S SEE IT IN ACTION, THEN IT'S OFF TO FISH WITH THE FAMILY!
IN ACTION! YES! AND NOTHING BAD WILL HAPPEN!
HEY, YOU GUYS GONNA COME SEE GYRO'S INVENTION SPIRAL OUT OF CONTROL?
I THINK WE'RE GONNA HANG BACK FOR A FEW.
I UNDERSTAND. THAT IMPOSSIBLY HUGE WATERMELON'S NOT GONNA WATCH ITSELF.

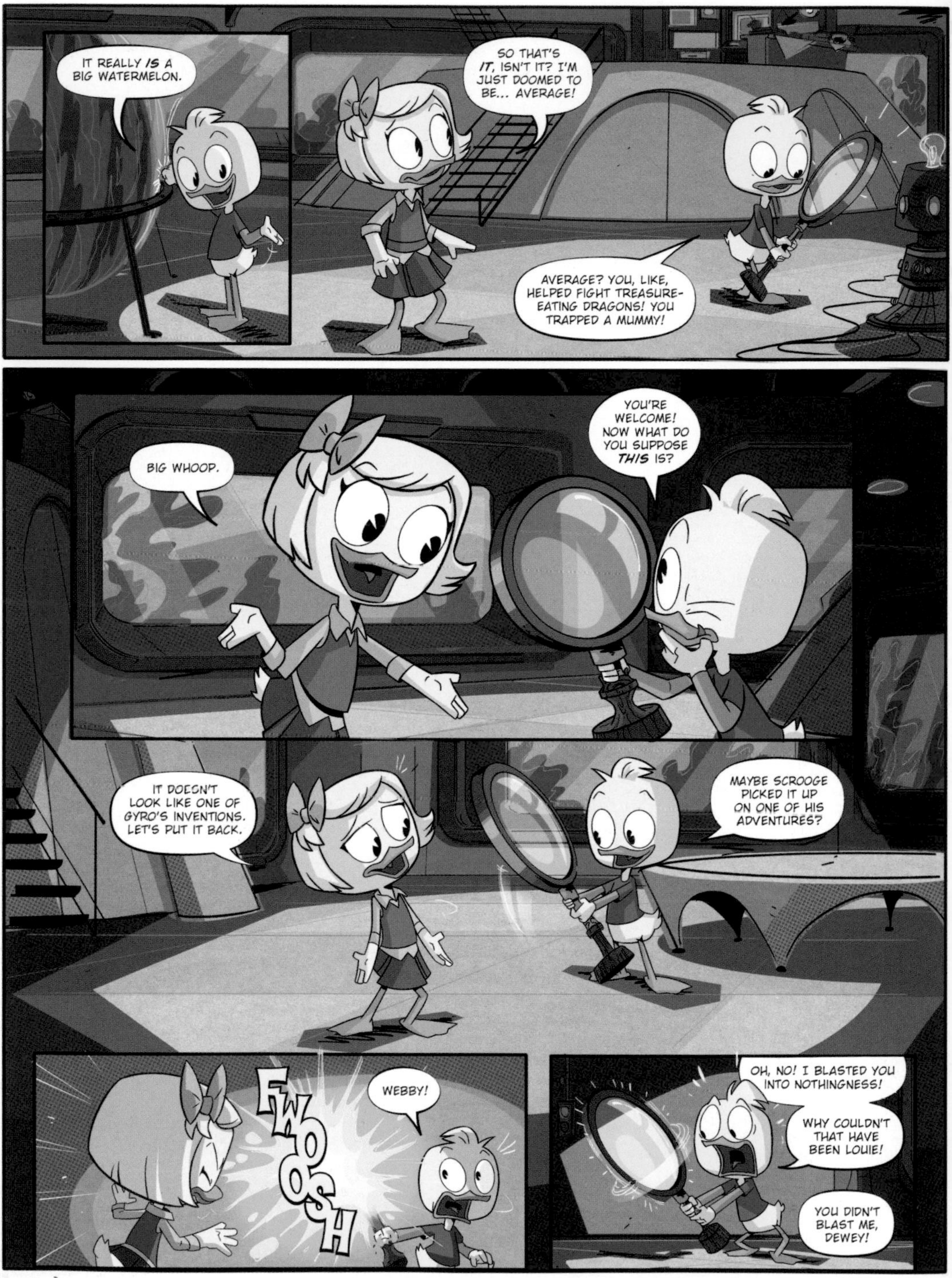
IT REALLY IS A BIG WATERMELON.
SO THAT'S IT, ISN'T IT? I'M JUST DOOMED TO BE... AVERAGE!
AVERAGE? YOU, LIKE, HELPED FIGHT TREASURE-EATING DRAGONS! YOU TRAPPED A MUMMY!
BIG WHOOP.
YOU'RE WELCOME! NOW WHAT DO YOU SUPPOSE THIS IS?
IT DOESN'T LOOK LIKE ONE OF GYRO'S INVENTIONS. LET'S PUT IT BACK.
MAYBE SCROOGE PICKED IT UP ON ONE OF HIS ADVENTURES?
FWOOSH
WEBBY!
OH, NO! I BLASTED YOU INTO NOTHINGNESS!
WHY COULDN'T THAT HAVE BEEN LOUIE!
YOU DIDN'T BLAST ME, DEWEY!

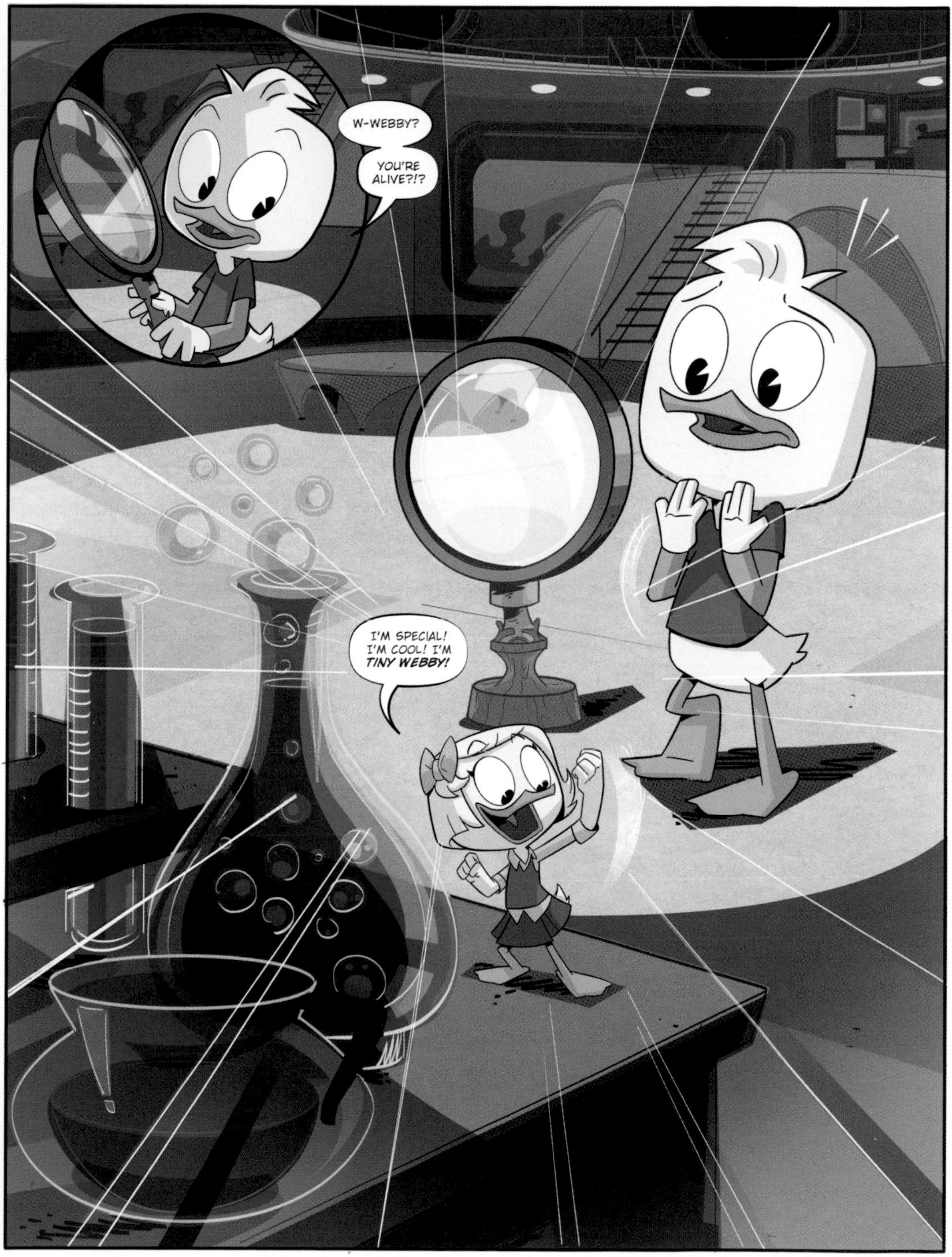
W-WEBBY?
YOU'RE ALIVE?!?
I'M SPECIAL! I'M COOL! I'M ***TINY WEBBY!***

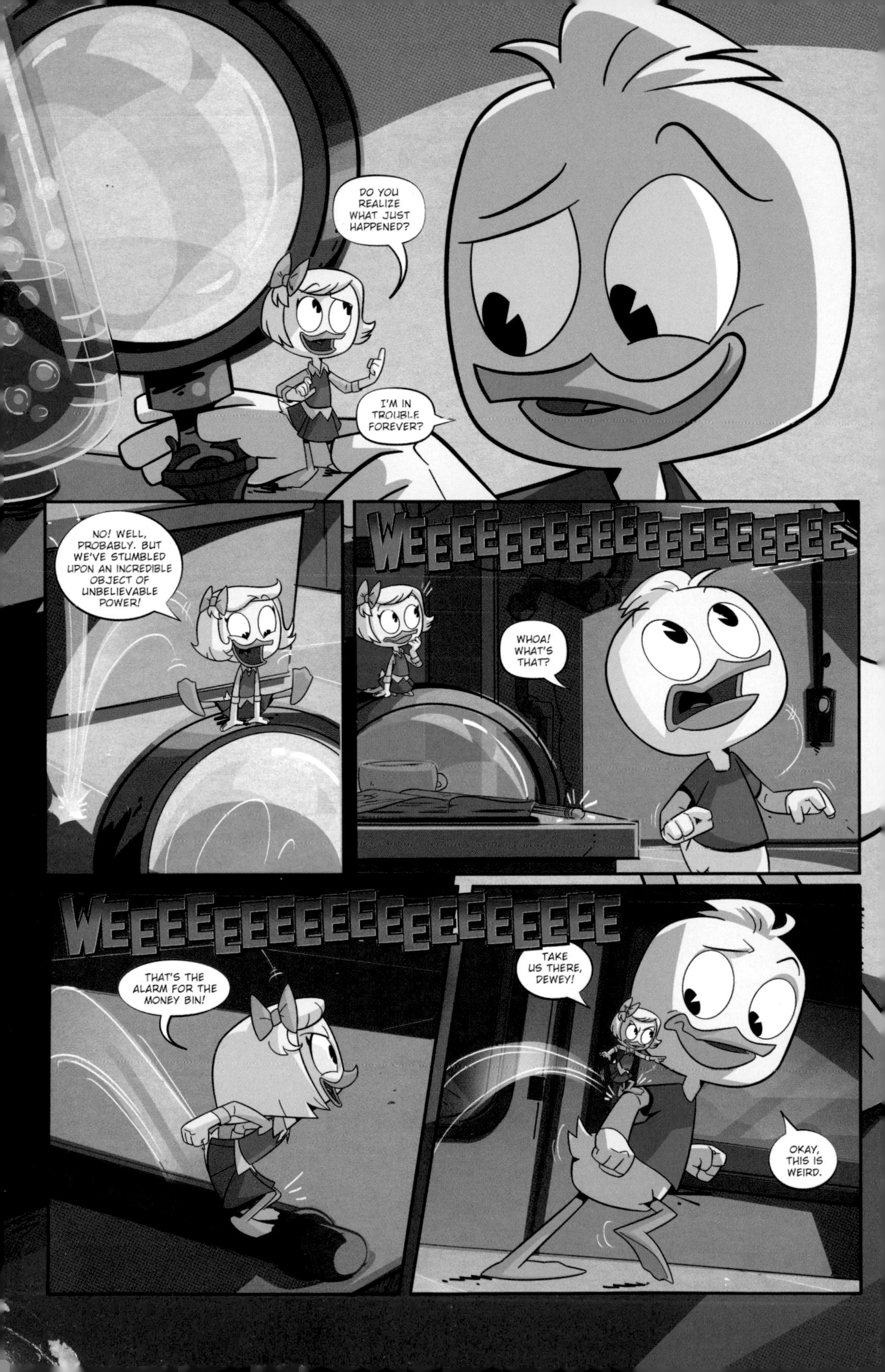
DO YOU REALIZE WHAT JUST HAPPENED?
I'M IN TROUBLE FOREVER?
NO! WELL, PROBABLY. BUT WE'VE STUMBLED UPON AN INCREDIBLE OBJECT OF UNBELIEVABLE POWER!
WEEEEEEEEEEEEEEEEEEE
WHOA! WHAT'S THAT?
WEEEEEEEEEEEEEEEEEEE
THAT'S THE ALARM FOR THE MONEY BIN!
TAKE US THERE, DEWEY!
OKAY, THIS IS WEIRD.

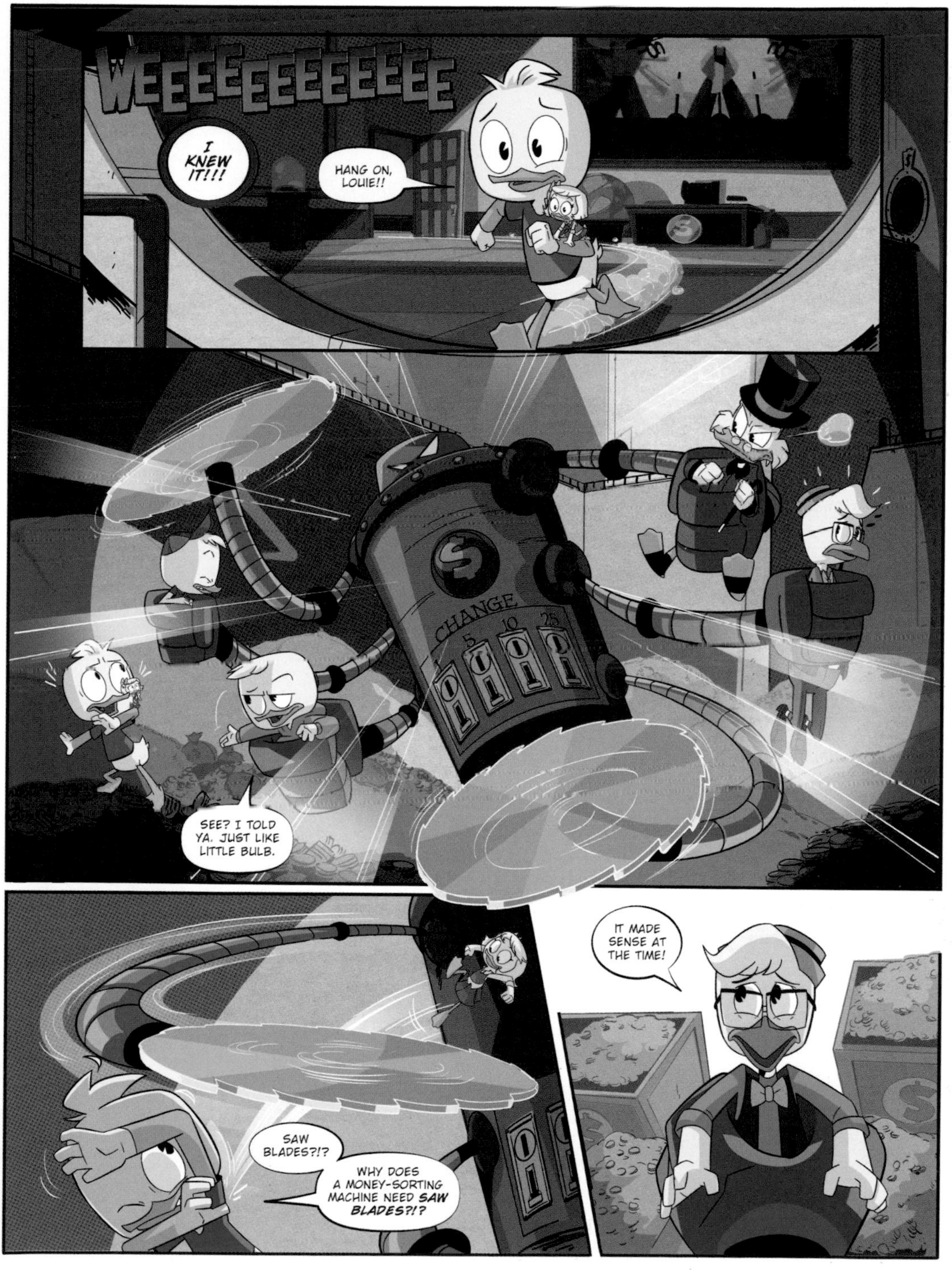
WEEEEEEEEEEEE
I KNEW IT!!!
HANG ON, LOUIE!!
CHANGE
5
10
25
SEE? I TOLD YA. JUST LIKE LITTLE BULB.
IT MADE SENSE AT THE TIME!
SAW BLADES?!?
WHY DOES A MONEY-SORTING MACHINE NEED SAW BLADES?!?

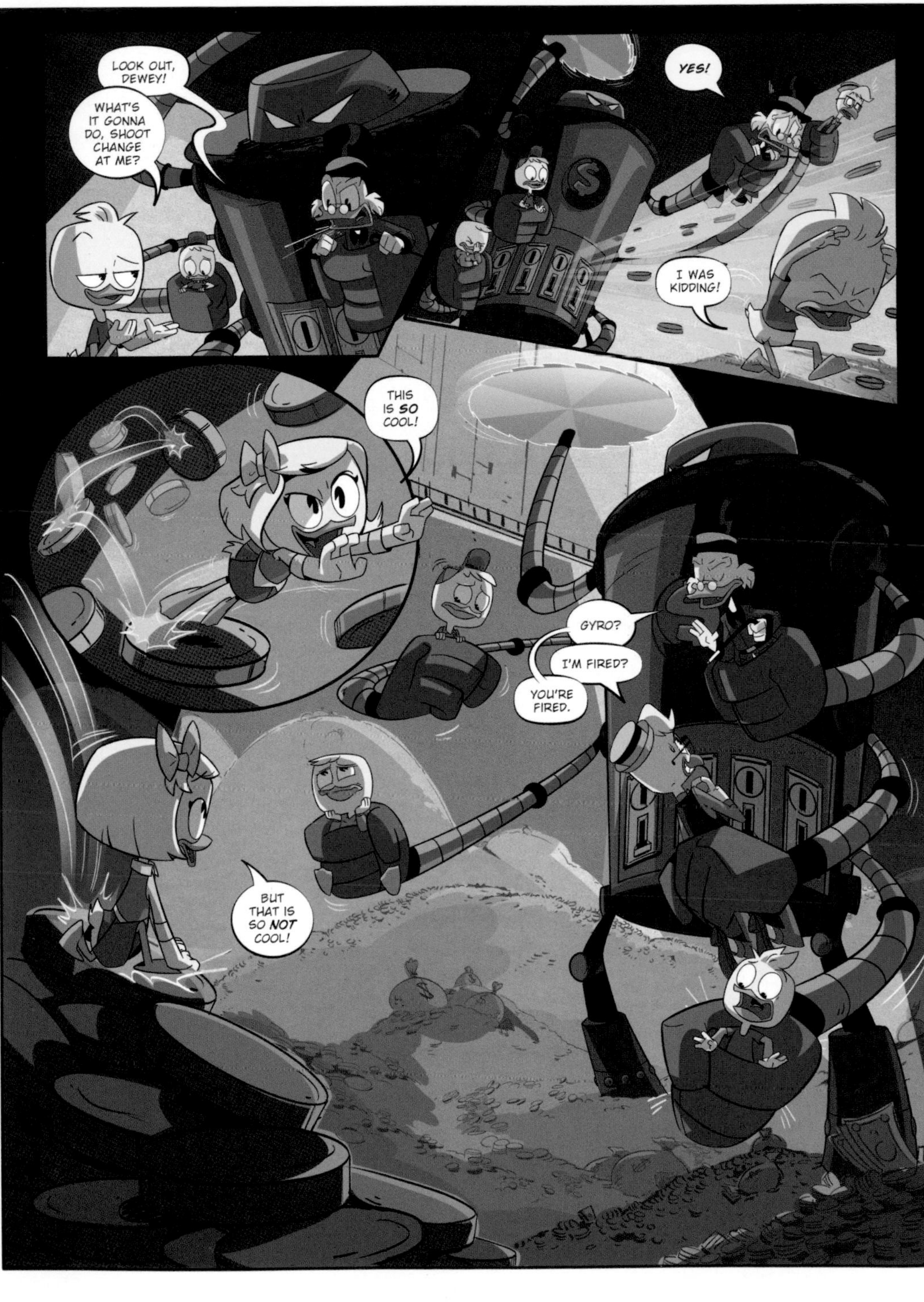
LOOK OUT, DEWEY!
WHAT'S IT GONNA DO, SHOOT CHANGE AT ME?
YES!
I WAS KIDDING!
THIS IS SO COOL!
GYRO?
I'M FIRED?
YOU'RE FIRED.
BUT THAT IS SO NOT COOL!

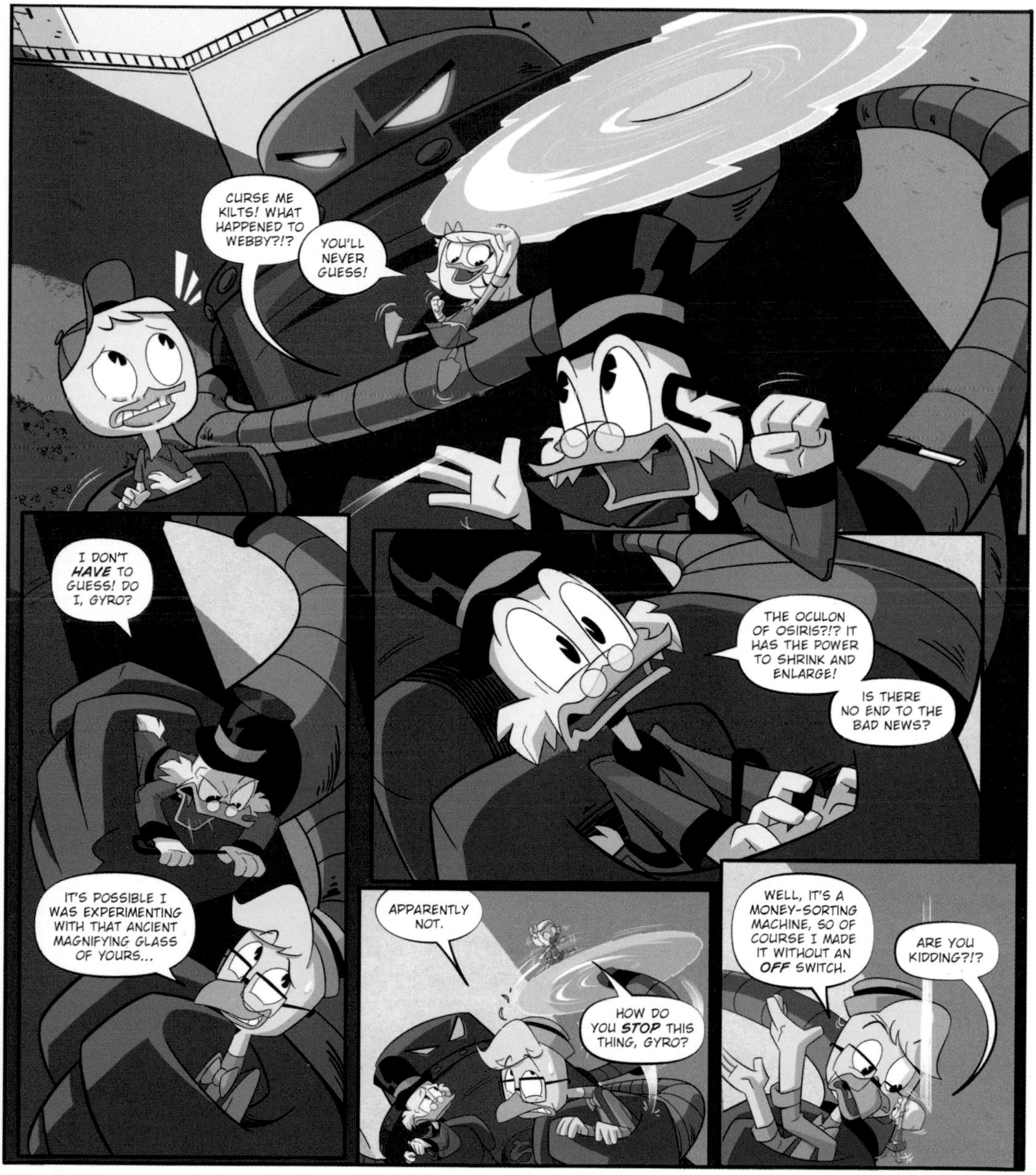
CURSE ME KILTS! WHAT HAPPENED TO WEBBY?!?
YOU'LL NEVER GUESS!
I DON'T **HAVE** TO GUESS! DO I, GYRO?
IT'S POSSIBLE I WAS EXPERIMENTING WITH THAT ANCIENT MAGNIFYING GLASS OF YOURS...
THE OCULON OF OSIRIS?!? IT HAS THE POWER TO SHRINK AND ENLARGE!
IS THERE NO END TO THE BAD NEWS?
APPARENTLY NOT.
HOW DO YOU **STOP** THIS THING, GYRO?
WELL, IT'S A MONEY-SORTING MACHINE, SO OF COURSE I MADE IT WITHOUT AN **OFF** SWITCH.
ARE YOU KIDDING?!?

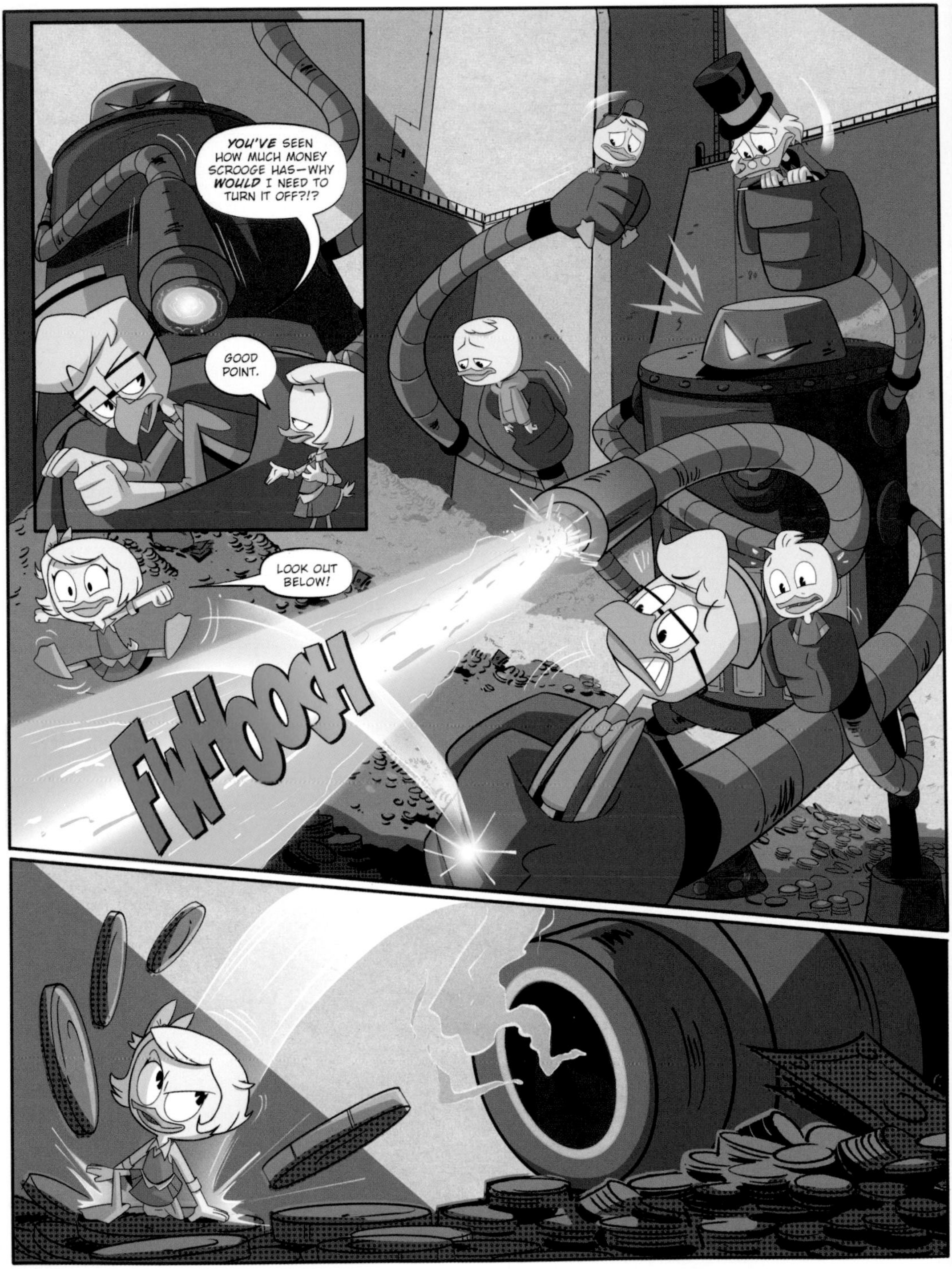
YOU'VE SEEN HOW MUCH MONEY SCROOGE HAS—WHY WOULD I NEED TO TURN IT OFF?!?
GOOD POINT.
LOOK OUT BELOW!
FWHOOSH

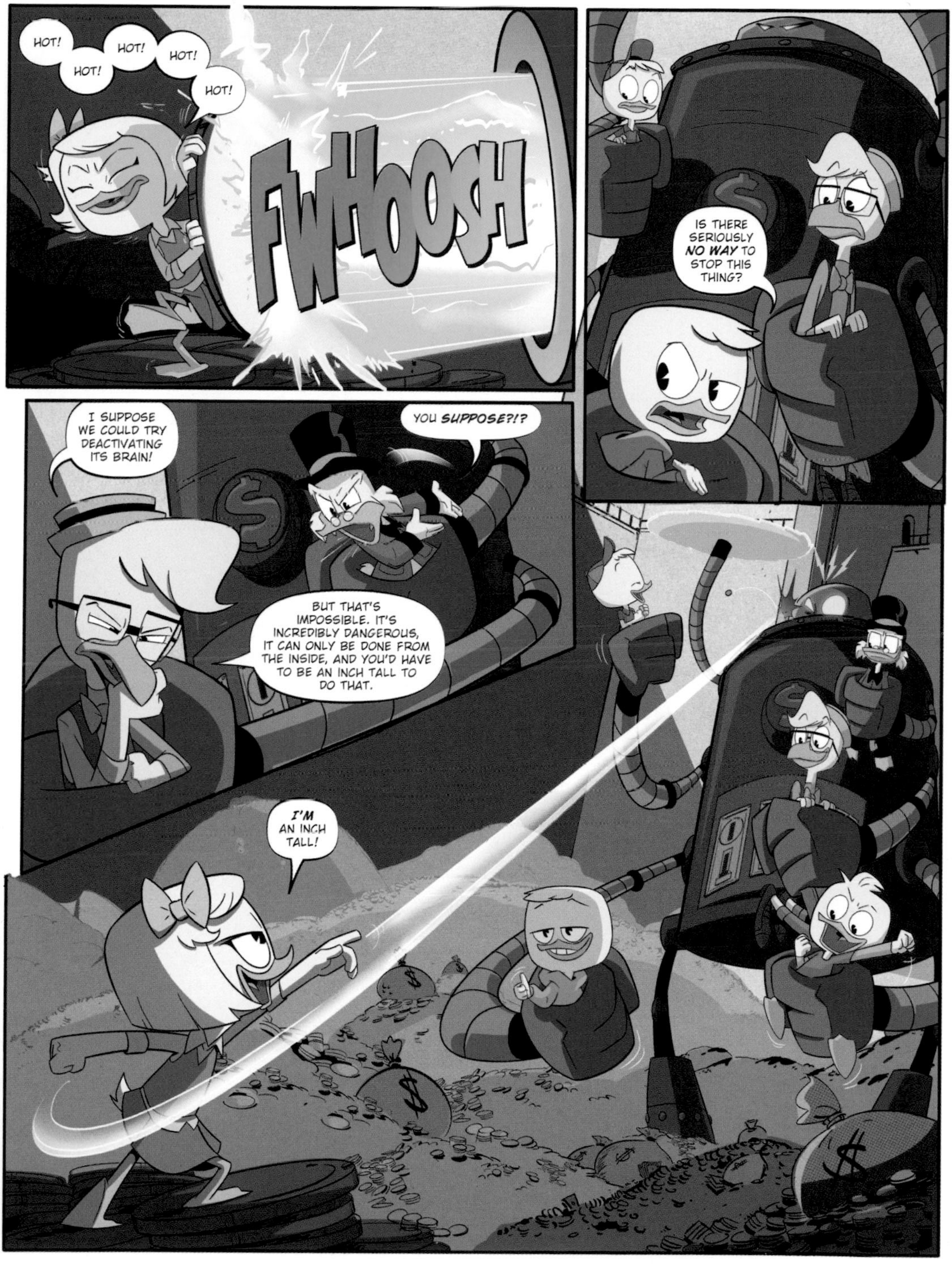
HOT!
HOT!
HOT!
HOT!
HOT!
FWHOOSH
IS THERE SERIOUSLY **NO WAY** TO STOP THIS THING?
I SUPPOSE WE COULD TRY DEACTIVATING ITS BRAIN!
YOU ***SUPPOSE?!?***
BUT THAT'S IMPOSSIBLE. IT'S INCREDIBLY DANGEROUS, IT CAN ONLY BE DONE FROM THE INSIDE, AND YOU'D HAVE TO BE AN INCH TALL TO DO THAT.
I'M AN INCH TALL!

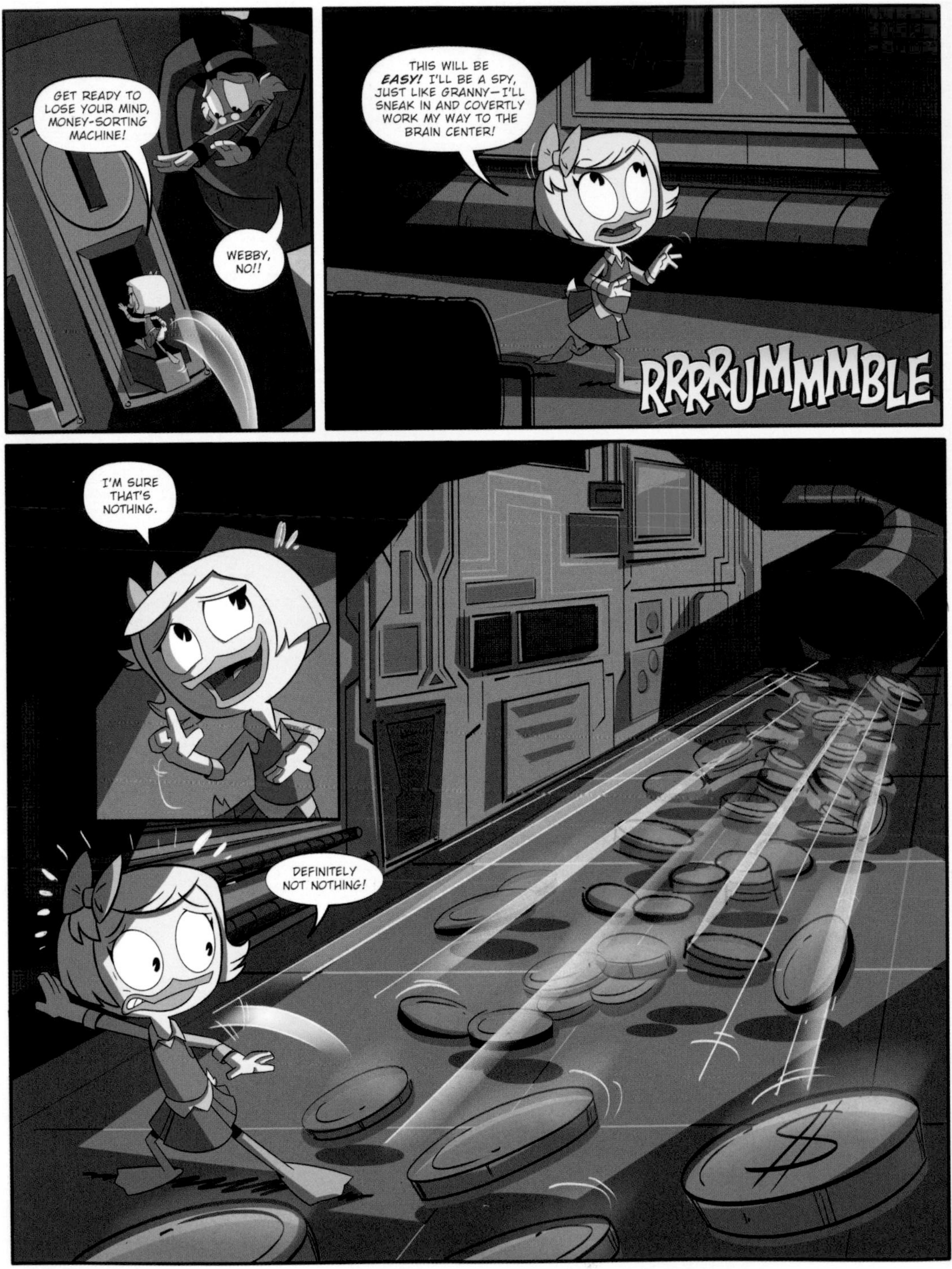
GET READY TO LOSE YOUR MIND, MONEY-SORTING MACHINE!
WEBBY, NO!!
THIS WILL BE EASY! I'LL BE A SPY, JUST LIKE GRANNY—I'LL SNEAK IN AND COVERTLY WORK MY WAY TO THE BRAIN CENTER!
RRRRUMMMBLE
I'M SURE THAT'S NOTHING.
DEFINITELY NOT NOTHING!

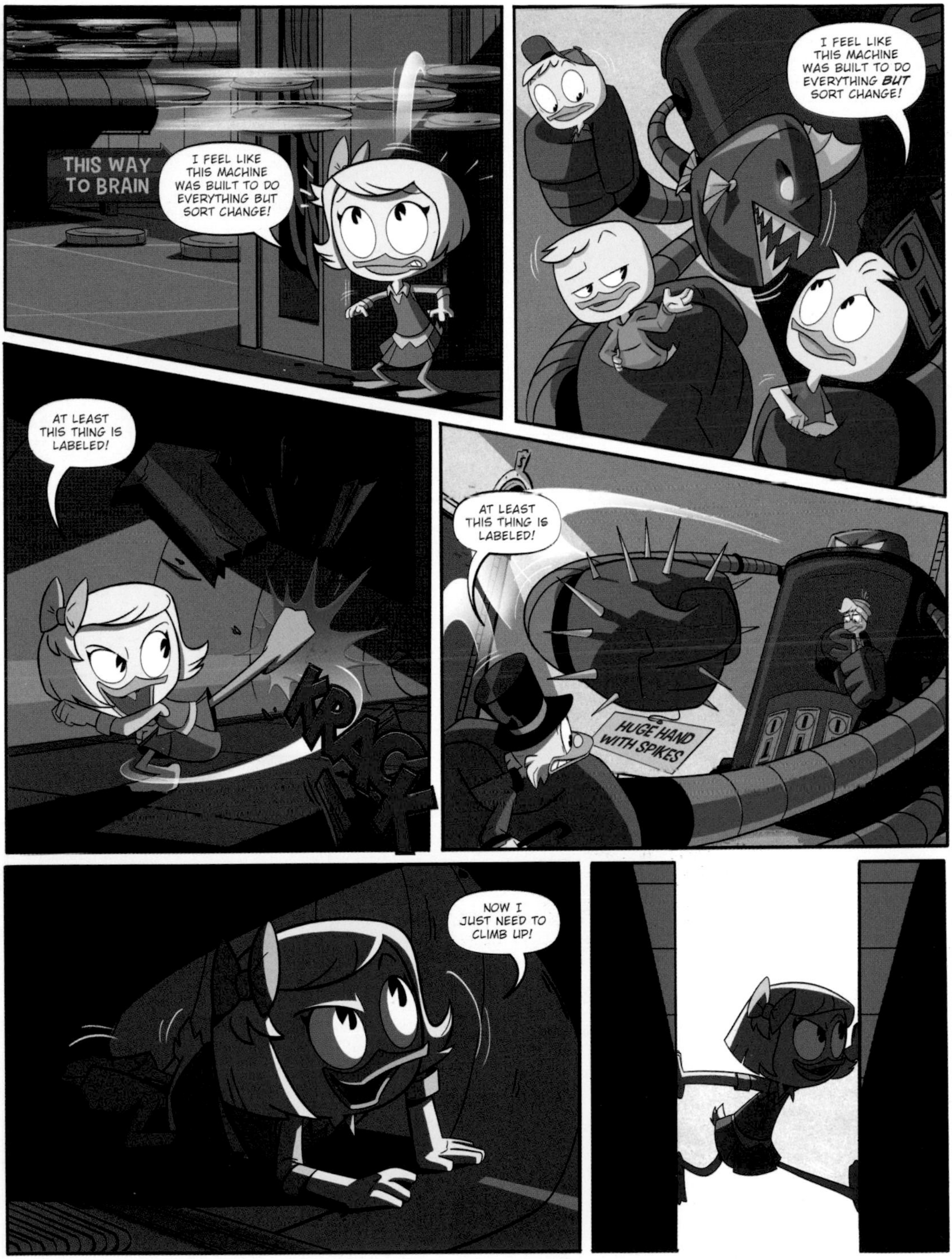
THIS WAY TO BRAIN
I FEEL LIKE THIS MACHINE WAS BUILT TO DO EVERYTHING BUT SORT CHANGE!
I FEEL LIKE THIS MACHINE WAS BUILT TO DO EVERYTHING BUT SORT CHANGE!
AT LEAST THIS THING IS LABELED!
KRACK
AT LEAST THIS THING IS LABELED!
HUGE HAND WITH SPIKES
NOW I JUST NEED TO CLIMB UP!

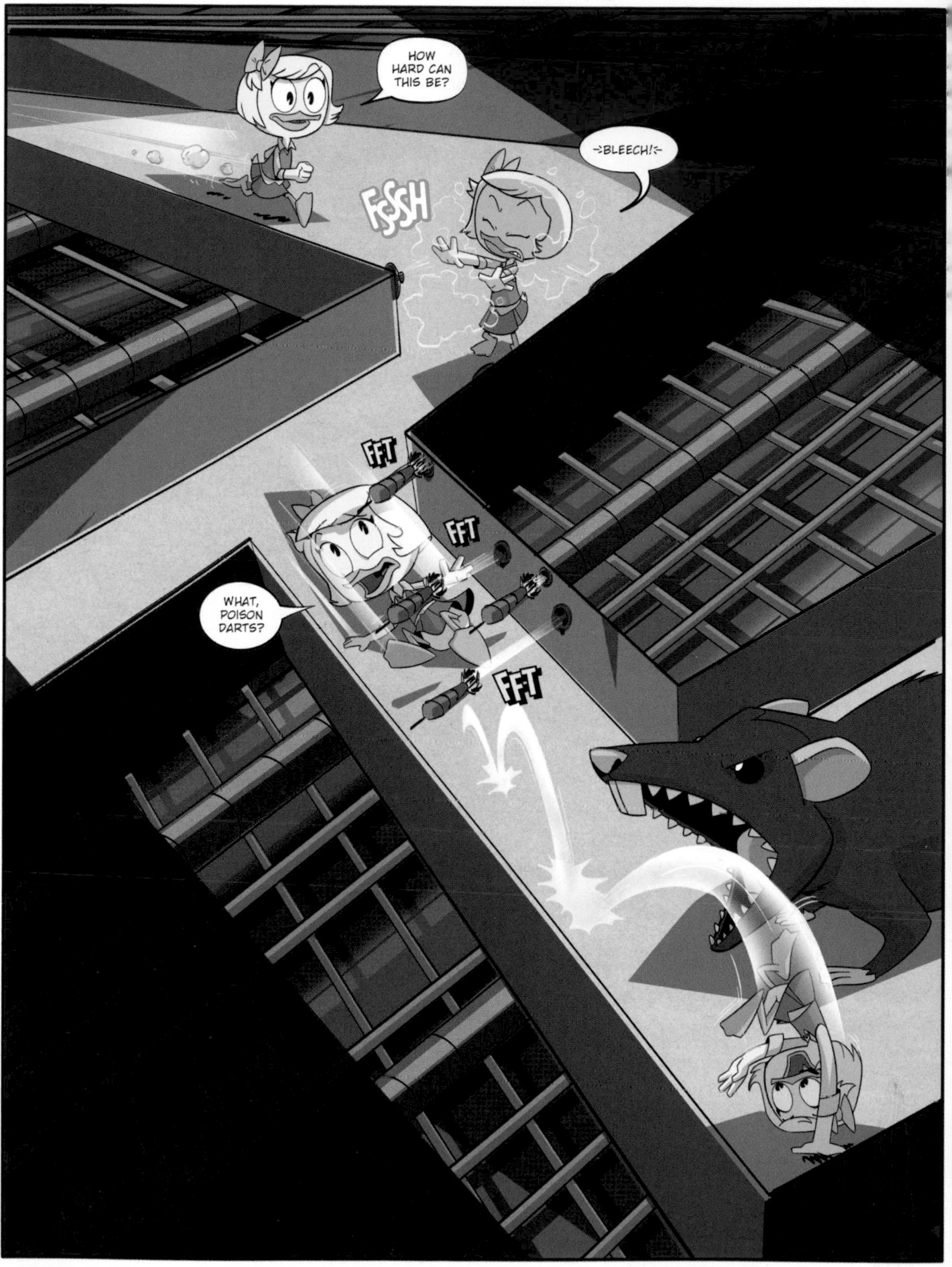
HOW HARD CAN THIS BE?
FSSSH
BLEECH!
FFT
FFT
WHAT, POISON DARTS?
FFT

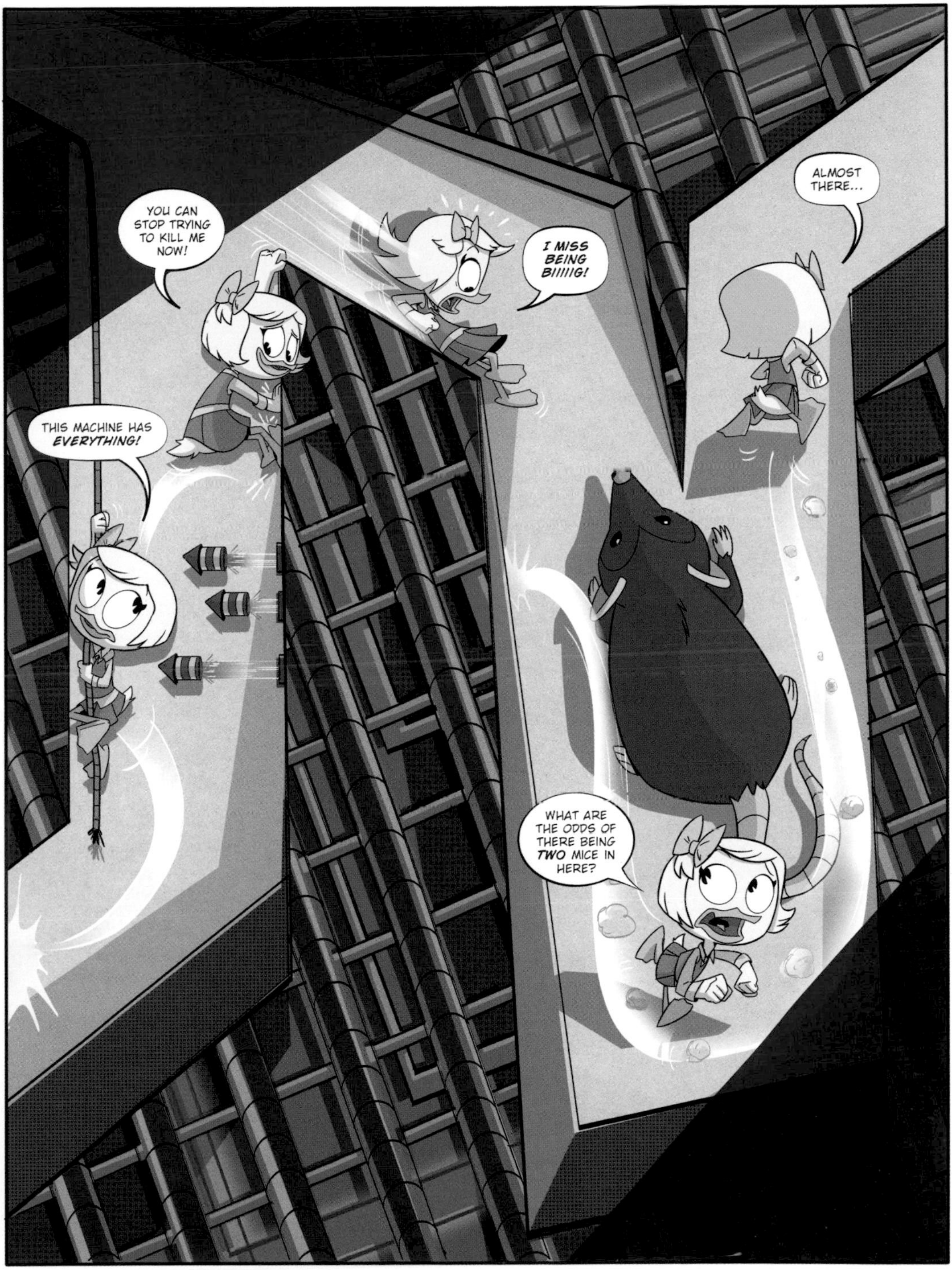
YOU CAN STOP TRYING TO KILL ME NOW!
I MISS BEING BIIIIIG!
ALMOST THERE...
THIS MACHINE HAS EVERYTHING!
WHAT ARE THE ODDS OF THERE BEING TWO MICE IN HERE?

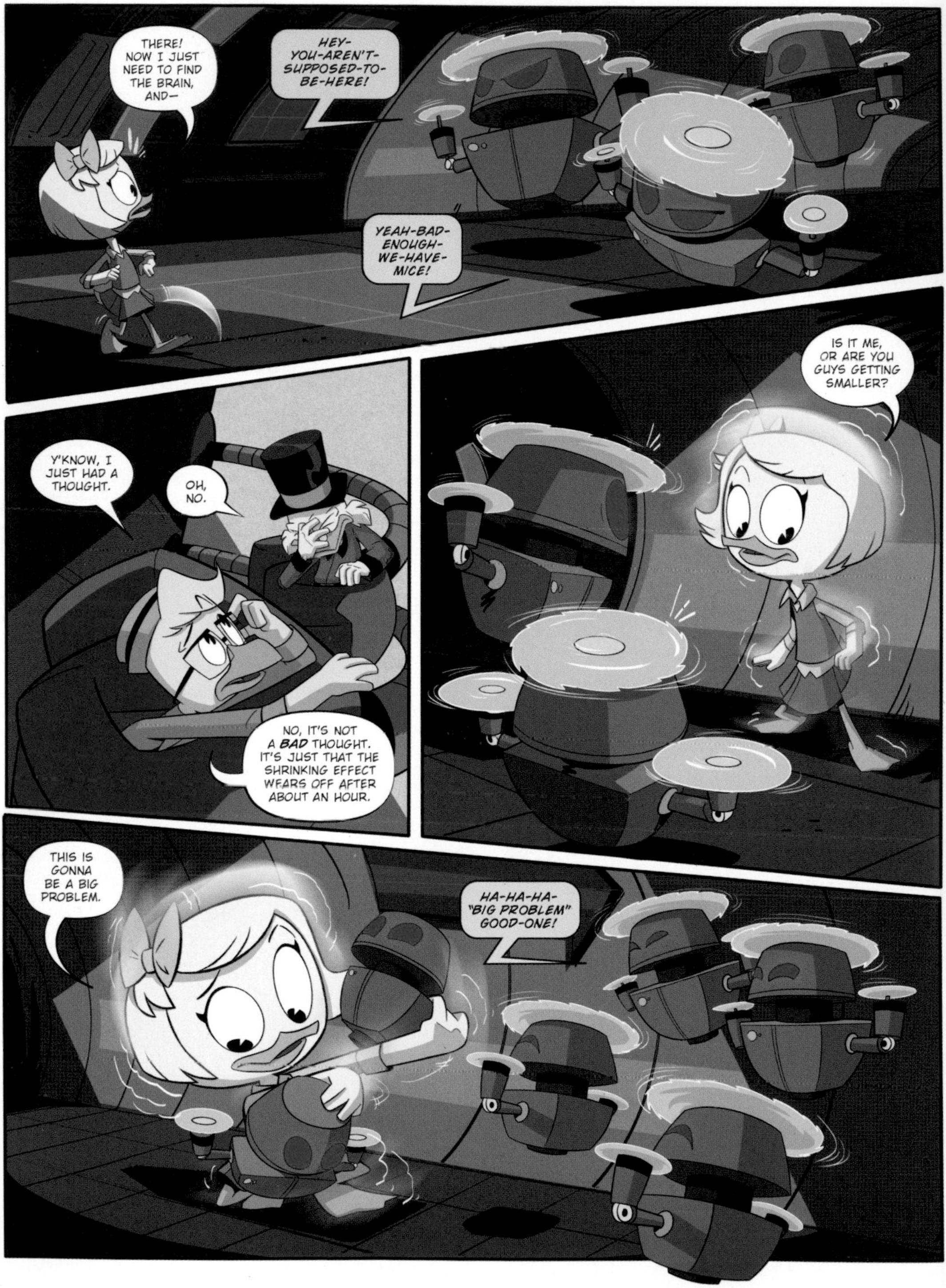
THERE! NOW I JUST NEED TO FIND THE BRAIN, AND—
HEY-YOU-AREN'T-SUPPOSED-TO-BE-HERE!
YEAH-BAD-ENOUGH-WE-HAVE-MICE!
Y'KNOW, I JUST HAD A THOUGHT.
OH, NO.
NO, IT'S NOT A BAD THOUGHT. IT'S JUST THAT THE SHRINKING EFFECT WEARS OFF AFTER ABOUT AN HOUR.
IS IT ME, OR ARE YOU GUYS GETTING SMALLER?
THIS IS GONNA BE A BIG PROBLEM.
HA-HA-HA-"BIG PROBLEM" GOOD-ONE!

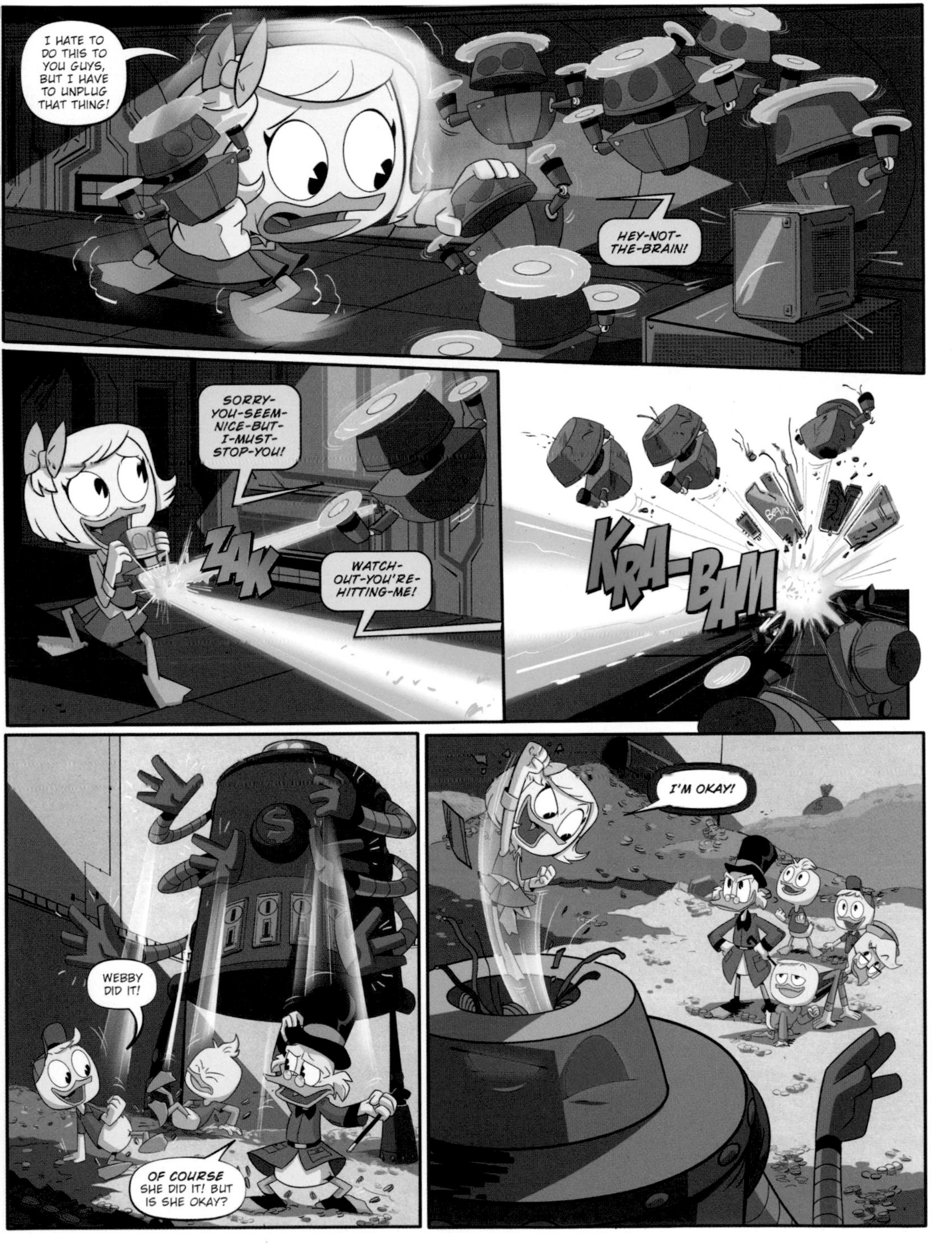
I HATE TO DO THIS TO YOU GUYS, BUT I HAVE TO UNPLUG THAT THING!
HEY-NOT-THE-BRAIN!
SORRY-YOU-SEEM-NICE-BUT-I-MUST-STOP-YOU!
ZAK
WATCH-OUT-YOU'RE-HITTING-ME!
KRA-BAM
WEBBY DID IT!
OF COURSE SHE DID IT! BUT IS SHE OKAY?
I'M OKAY!

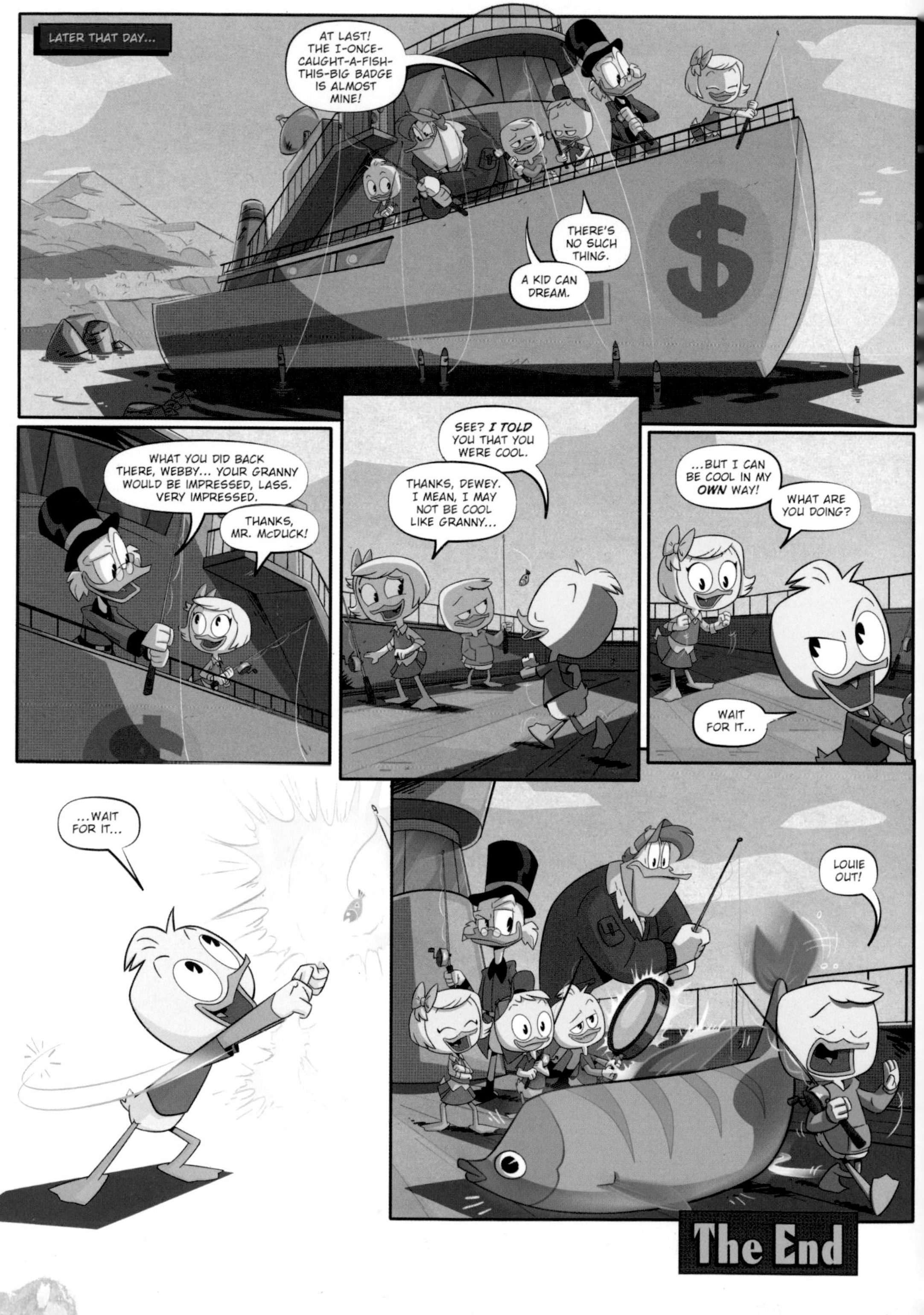

LATER THAT DAY...
AT LAST! THE I-ONCE-CAUGHT-A-FISH-THIS-BIG BADGE IS ALMOST MINE!
THERE'S NO SUCH THING.
A KID CAN DREAM.
WHAT YOU DID BACK THERE, WEBBY... YOUR GRANNY WOULD BE IMPRESSED, LASS. VERY IMPRESSED.
THANKS, MR. McDUCK!
SEE? I TOLD YOU THAT YOU WERE COOL.
THANKS, DEWEY. I MEAN, I MAY NOT BE COOL LIKE GRANNY...
...BUT I CAN BE COOL IN MY OWN WAY!
WHAT ARE YOU DOING?
WAIT FOR IT...
...WAIT FOR IT...
LOUIE OUT!
The End

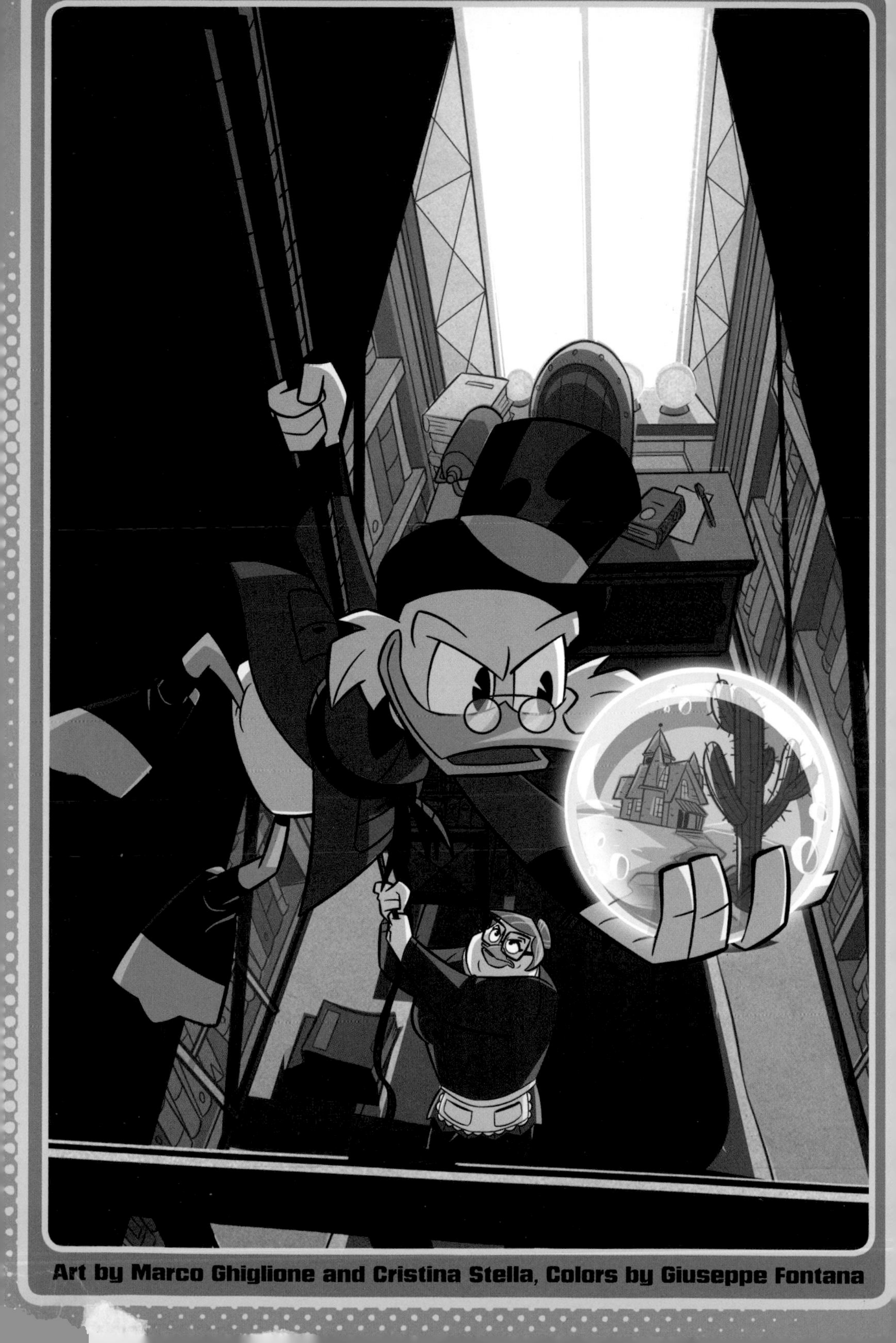

Art by Marco Ghiglione and Cristina Stella, Colors by Giuseppe Fontana

Disney DuckTales

MAROONED IN MYSTERY MANSION!

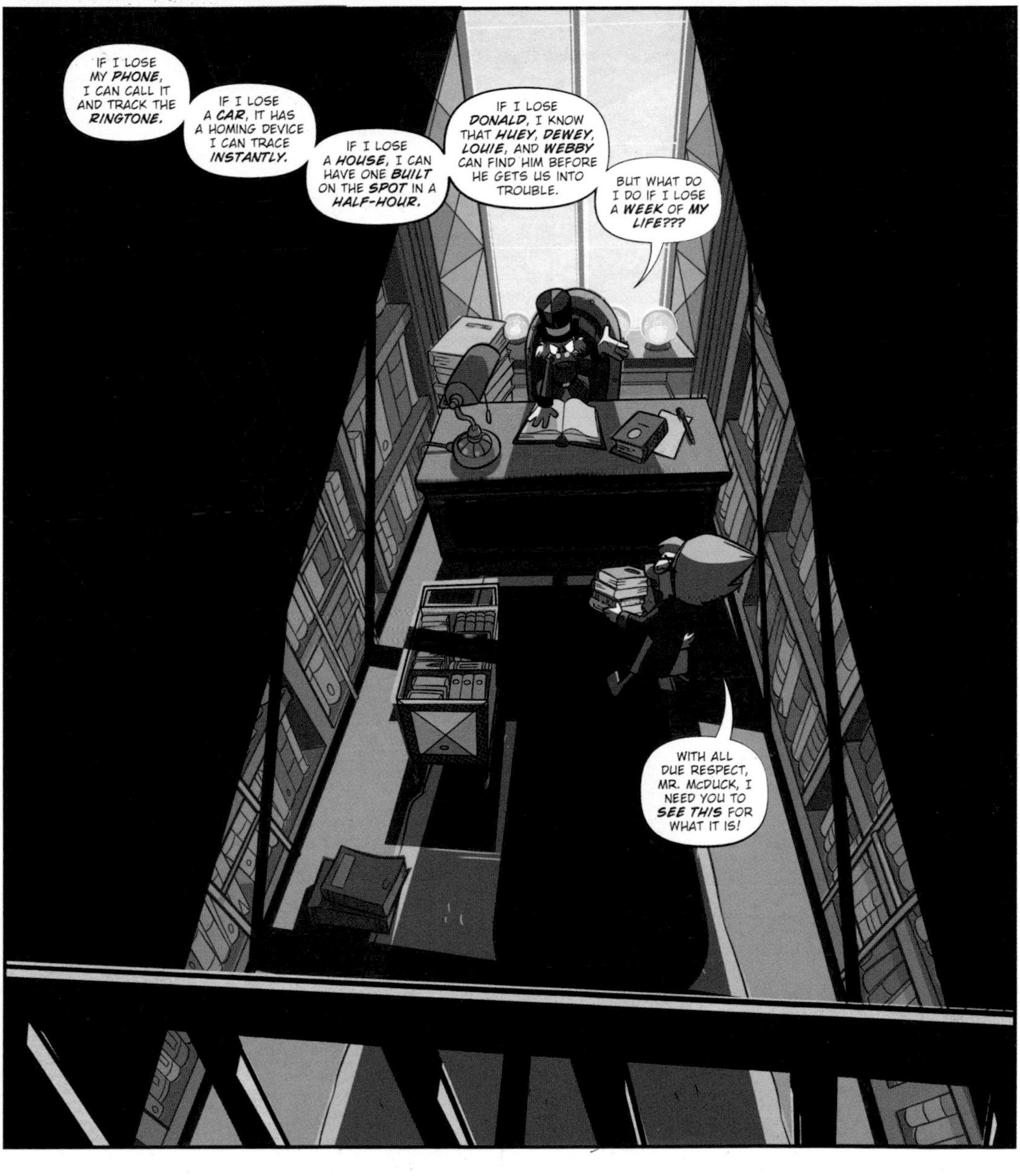

IF I LOSE MY PHONE, I CAN CALL IT AND TRACK THE RINGTONE.
IF I LOSE A CAR, IT HAS A HOMING DEVICE I CAN TRACE INSTANTLY.
IF I LOSE A HOUSE, I CAN HAVE ONE BUILT ON THE SPOT IN A HALF-HOUR.
IF I LOSE DONALD, I KNOW THAT HUEY, DEWEY, LOUIE, AND WEBBY CAN FIND HIM BEFORE HE GETS US INTO TROUBLE.
BUT WHAT DO I DO IF I LOSE A WEEK OF MY LIFE???
WITH ALL DUE RESPECT, MR. McDUCK, I NEED YOU TO SEE THIS FOR WHAT IT IS!

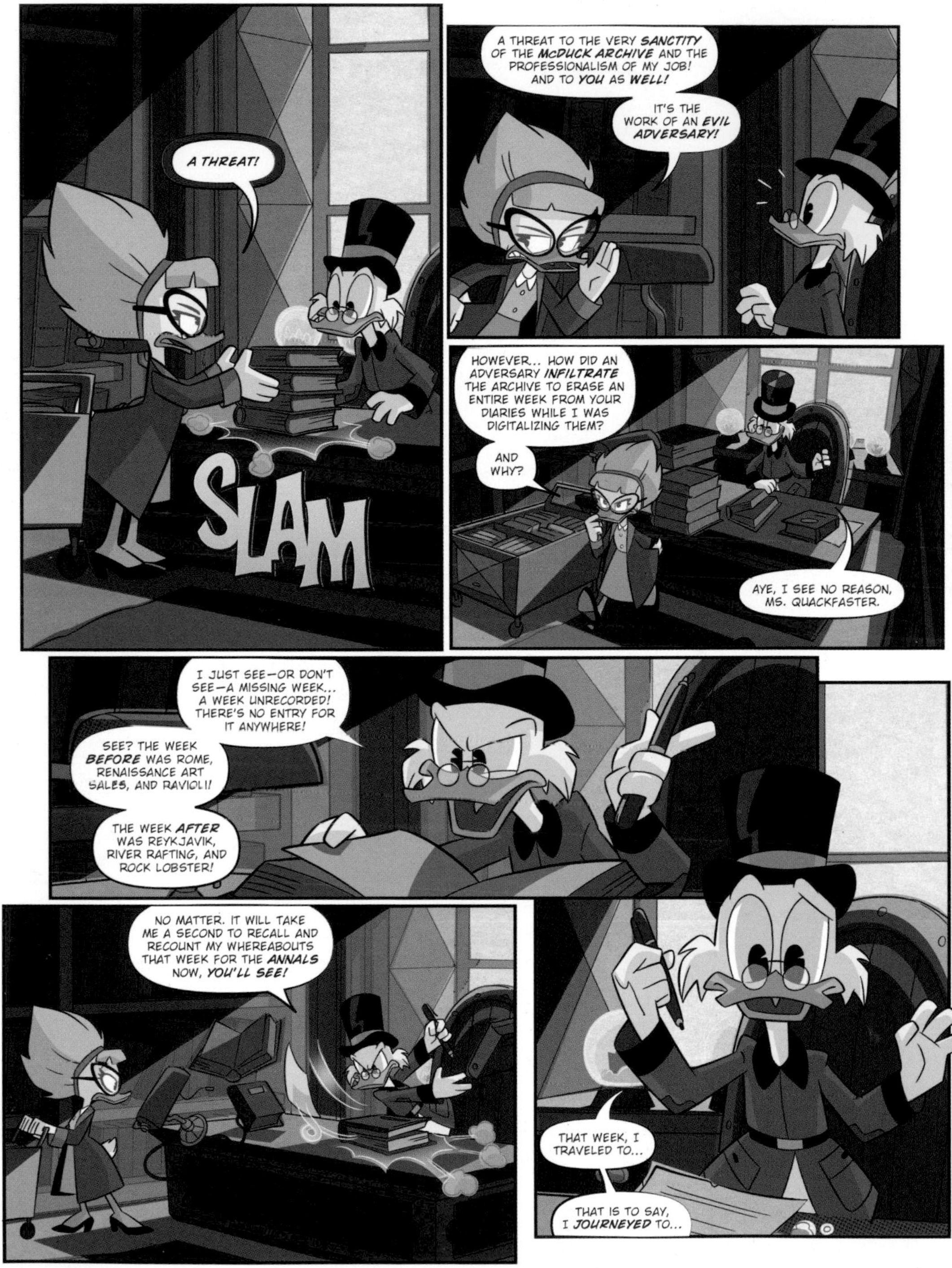
A THREAT!
SLAM
A THREAT TO THE VERY SANCTITY OF THE McDUCK ARCHIVE AND THE PROFESSIONALISM OF MY JOB! AND TO YOU AS WELL!
IT'S THE WORK OF AN EVIL ADVERSARY!
HOWEVER... HOW DID AN ADVERSARY INFILTRATE THE ARCHIVE TO ERASE AN ENTIRE WEEK FROM YOUR DIARIES WHILE I WAS DIGITALIZING THEM?
AND WHY?
AYE, I SEE NO REASON, MS. QUACKFASTER.
I JUST SEE—OR DON'T SEE—A MISSING WEEK... A WEEK UNRECORDED! THERE'S NO ENTRY FOR IT ANYWHERE!
SEE? THE WEEK BEFORE WAS ROME, RENAISSANCE ART SALES, AND RAVIOLI!
THE WEEK AFTER WAS REYKJAVIK, RIVER RAFTING, AND ROCK LOBSTER!
NO MATTER. IT WILL TAKE ME A SECOND TO RECALL AND RECOUNT MY WHEREABOUTS THAT WEEK FOR THE ANNALS NOW, YOU'LL SEE!
THAT WEEK, I TRAVELED TO...
THAT IS TO SAY, I JOURNEYED TO...

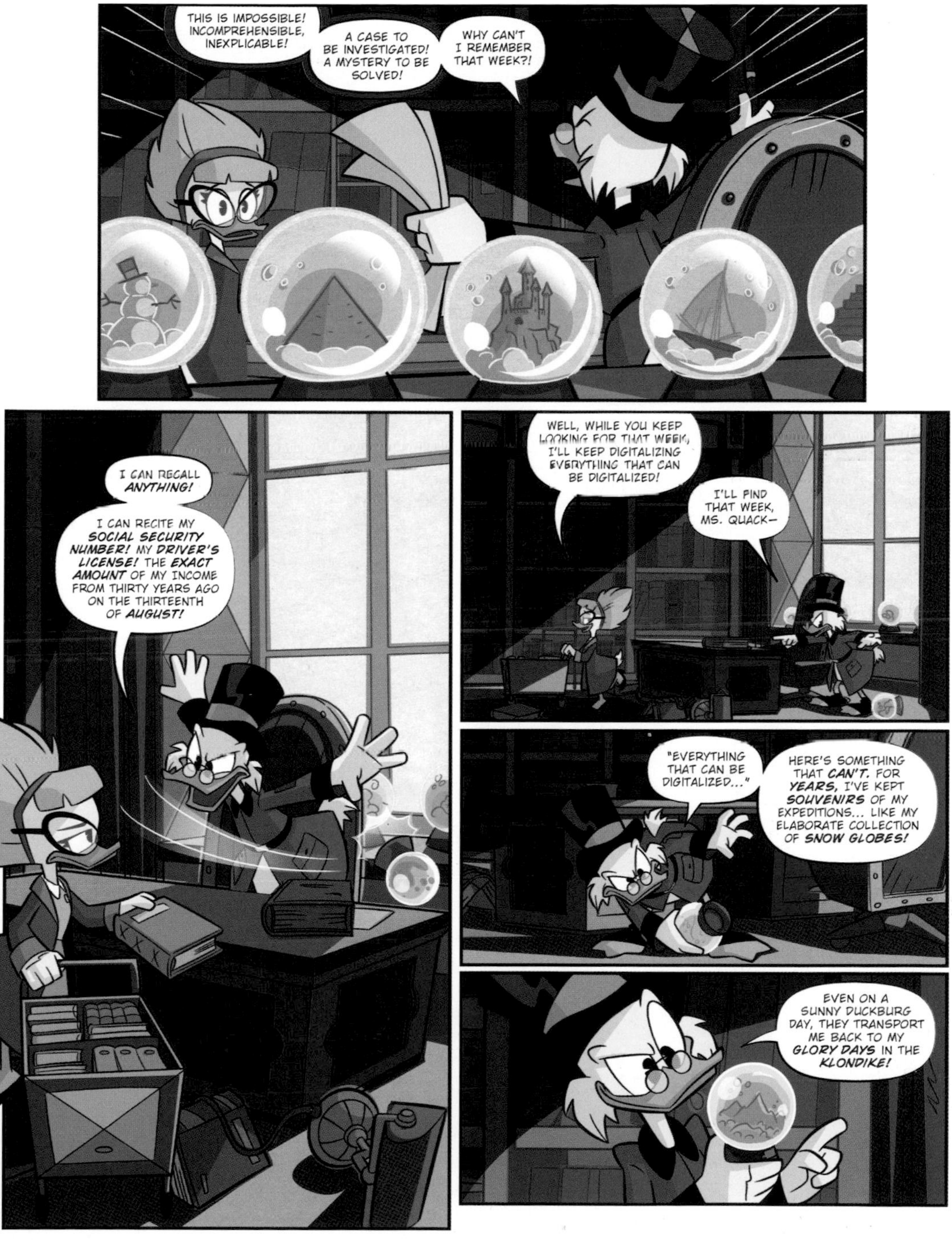
THIS IS IMPOSSIBLE! INCOMPREHENSIBLE, INEXPLICABLE!
A CASE TO BE INVESTIGATED! A MYSTERY TO BE SOLVED!
WHY CAN'T I REMEMBER THAT WEEK?!
I CAN RECALL ANYTHING!
I CAN RECITE MY SOCIAL SECURITY NUMBER! MY DRIVER'S LICENSE! THE EXACT AMOUNT OF MY INCOME FROM THIRTY YEARS AGO ON THE THIRTEENTH OF AUGUST!
WELL, WHILE YOU KEEP LOOKING FOR THAT WEEK, I'LL KEEP DIGITALIZING EVERYTHING THAT CAN BE DIGITALIZED!
I'LL FIND THAT WEEK, MS. QUACK—
"EVERYTHING THAT CAN BE DIGITALIZED..."
HERE'S SOMETHING THAT CAN'T. FOR YEARS, I'VE KEPT SOUVENIRS OF MY EXPEDITIONS... LIKE MY ELABORATE COLLECTION OF SNOW GLOBES!
EVEN ON A SUNNY DUCKBURG DAY, THEY TRANSPORT ME BACK TO MY GLORY DAYS IN THE KLONDIKE!

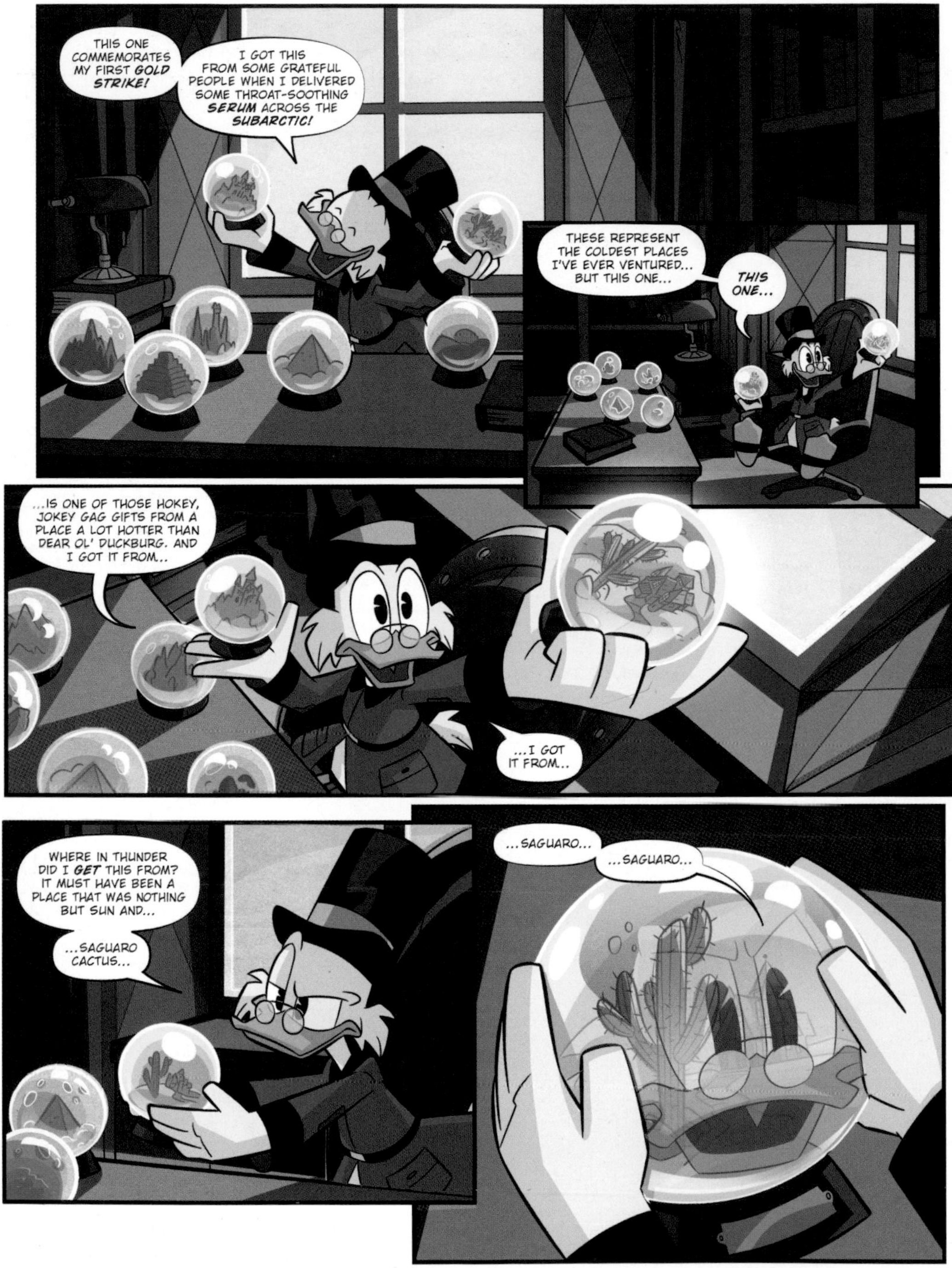
THIS ONE COMMEMORATES MY FIRST GOLD STRIKE!
I GOT THIS FROM SOME GRATEFUL PEOPLE WHEN I DELIVERED SOME THROAT-SOOTHING SERUM ACROSS THE SUBARCTIC!
THESE REPRESENT THE COLDEST PLACES I'VE EVER VENTURED... BUT THIS ONE...
THIS ONE...
...IS ONE OF THOSE HOKEY, JOKEY GAG GIFTS FROM A PLACE A LOT HOTTER THAN DEAR OL' DUCKBURG. AND I GOT IT FROM...
...I GOT IT FROM...
WHERE IN THUNDER DID I GET THIS FROM? IT MUST HAVE BEEN A PLACE THAT WAS NOTHING BUT SUN AND...
...SAGUARO CACTUS...
...SAGUARO...
...SAGUARO...

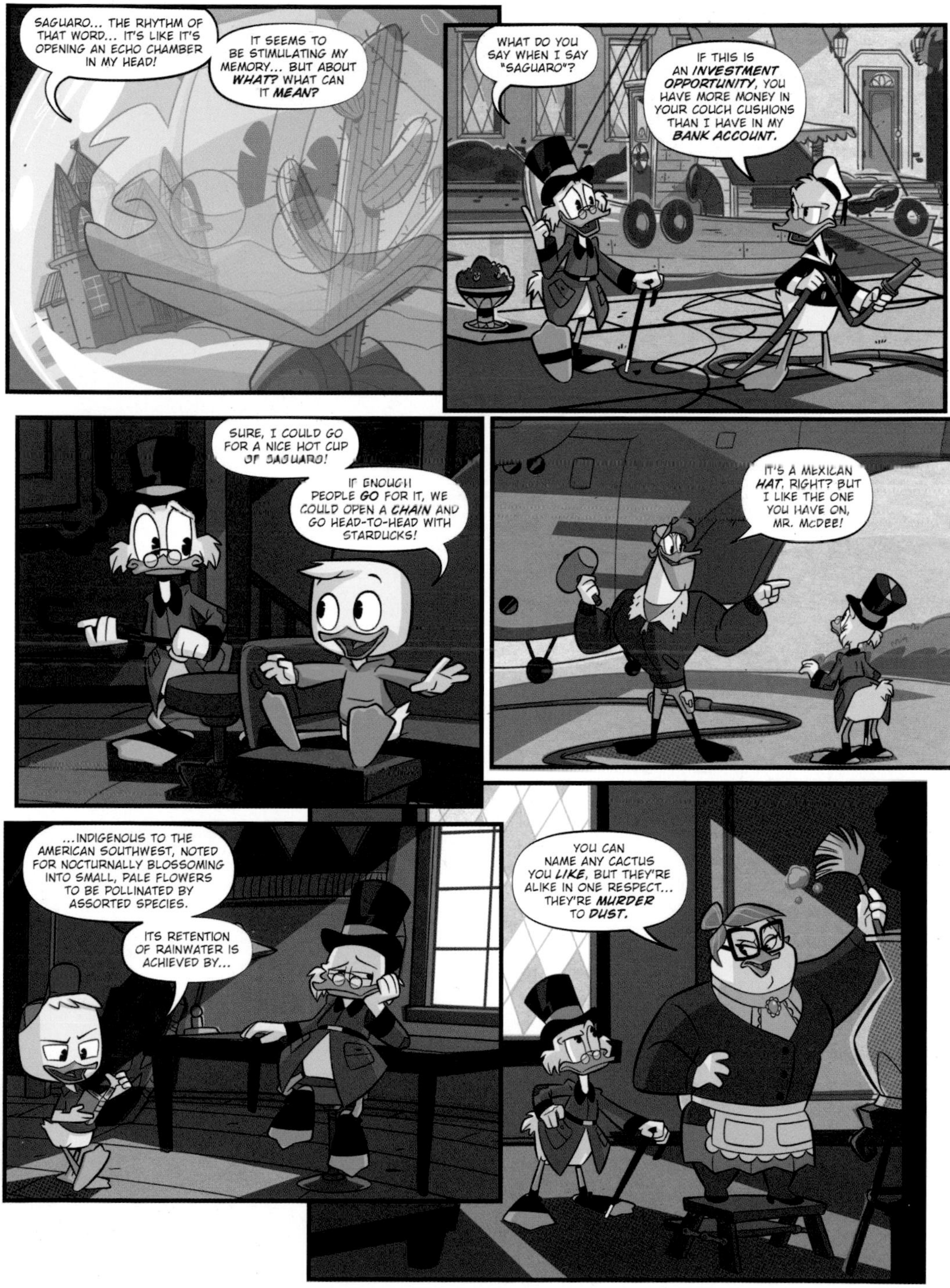
SAGUARO... THE RHYTHM OF THAT WORD... IT'S LIKE IT'S OPENING AN ECHO CHAMBER IN MY HEAD!
IT SEEMS TO BE STIMULATING MY MEMORY... BUT ABOUT **WHAT?** WHAT CAN IT **MEAN?**
WHAT DO YOU SAY WHEN I SAY "SAGUARO"?
IF THIS IS AN **INVESTMENT OPPORTUNITY**, YOU HAVE MORE MONEY IN YOUR COUCH CUSHIONS THAN I HAVE IN MY **BANK ACCOUNT.**
SURE, I COULD GO FOR A NICE HOT CUP OF SAGUARO!
IF ENOUGH PEOPLE **GO** FOR IT, WE COULD OPEN A **CHAIN** AND GO HEAD-TO-HEAD WITH STARDUCKS!
IT'S A MEXICAN **HAT**, RIGHT? BUT I LIKE THE ONE YOU HAVE ON, MR. McDEE!
...INDIGENOUS TO THE AMERICAN SOUTHWEST, NOTED FOR NOCTURNALLY BLOSSOMING INTO SMALL, PALE FLOWERS TO BE POLLINATED BY ASSORTED SPECIES.
ITS RETENTION OF RAINWATER IS ACHIEVED BY...
YOU CAN NAME ANY CACTUS YOU **LIKE**, BUT THEY'RE ALIKE IN ONE RESPECT... THEY'RE **MURDER** TO **DUST.**

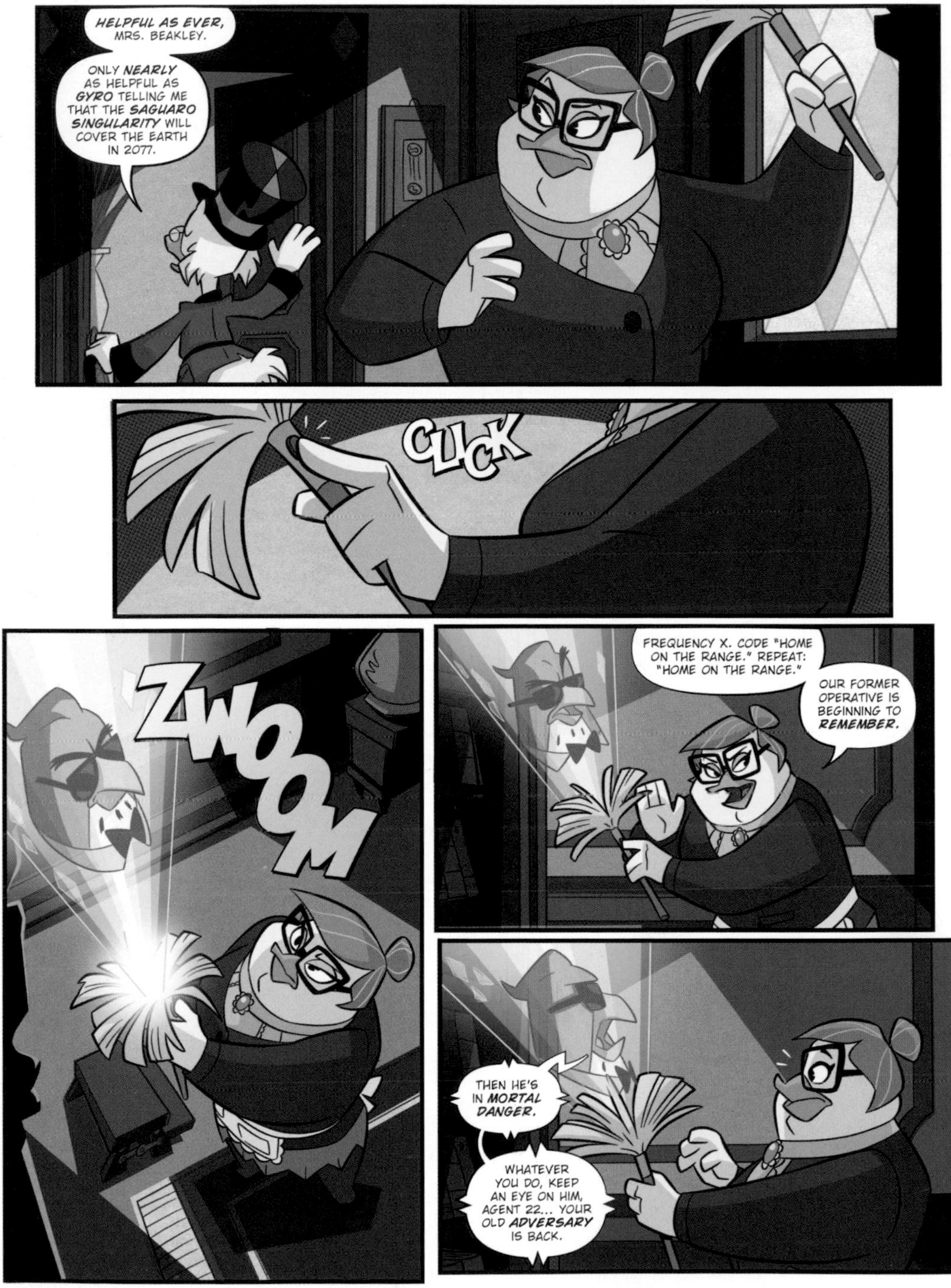
HELPFUL AS EVER, MRS. BEAKLEY.
ONLY NEARLY AS HELPFUL AS GYRO TELLING ME THAT THE SAGUARO SINGULARITY WILL COVER THE EARTH IN 2077.
CLICK
ZWOOM
FREQUENCY X. CODE "HOME ON THE RANGE." REPEAT: "HOME ON THE RANGE."
OUR FORMER OPERATIVE IS BEGINNING TO REMEMBER.
THEN HE'S IN MORTAL DANGER.
WHATEVER YOU DO, KEEP AN EYE ON HIM, AGENT 22... YOUR OLD ADVERSARY IS BACK.

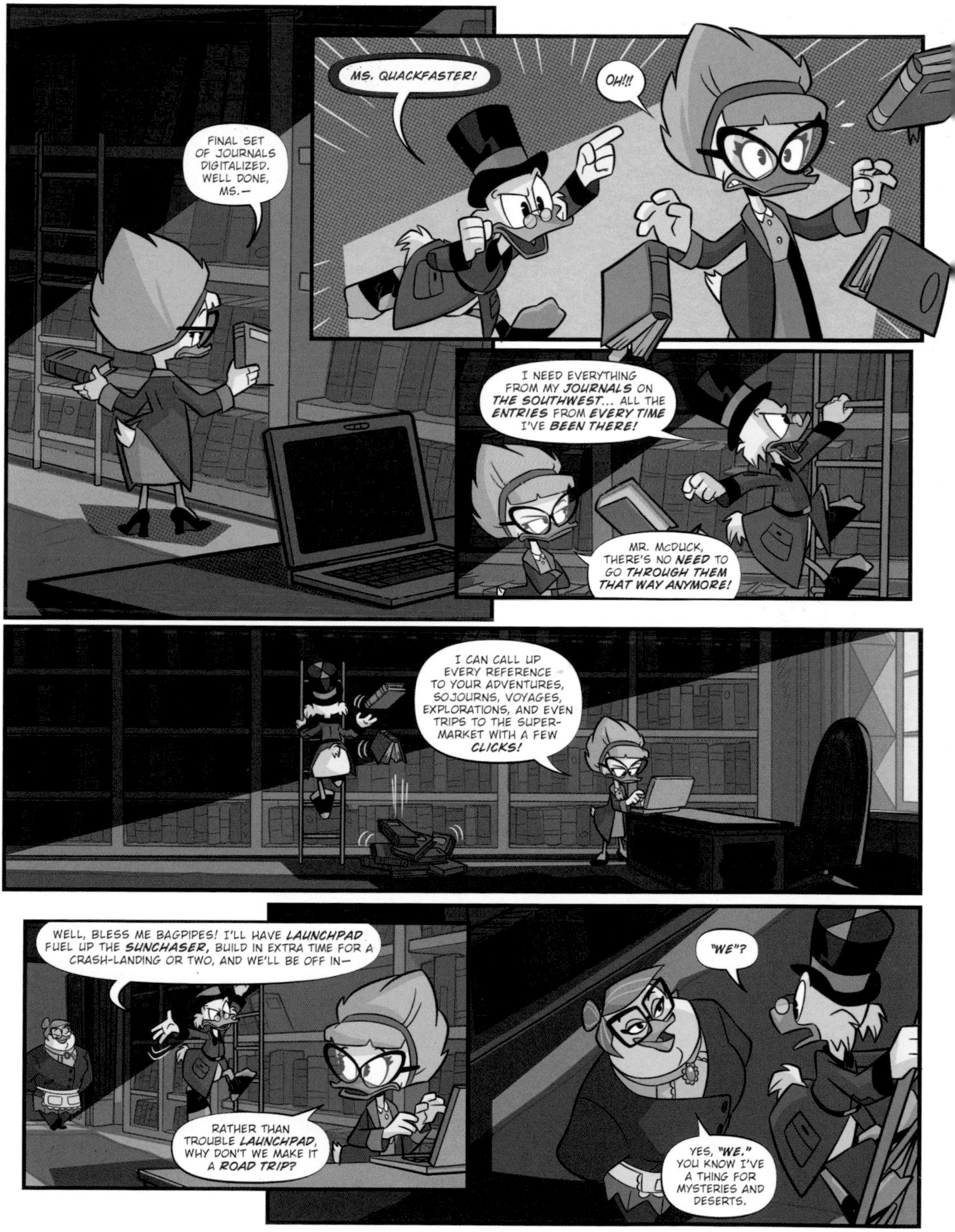
FINAL SET OF JOURNALS DIGITALIZED. WELL DONE, MS.—
MS. QUACKFASTER!
OH!!!
I NEED EVERYTHING FROM MY JOURNALS ON THE SOUTHWEST... ALL THE ENTRIES FROM EVERY TIME I'VE BEEN THERE!
MR. McDUCK, THERE'S NO NEED TO GO THROUGH THEM THAT WAY ANYMORE!
I CAN CALL UP EVERY REFERENCE TO YOUR ADVENTURES, SOJOURNS, VOYAGES, EXPLORATIONS, AND EVEN TRIPS TO THE SUPER-MARKET WITH A FEW CLICKS!
WELL, BLESS ME BAGPIPES! I'LL HAVE LAUNCHPAD FUEL UP THE SUNCHASER, BUILD IN EXTRA TIME FOR A CRASH-LANDING OR TWO, AND WE'LL BE OFF IN—
RATHER THAN TROUBLE LAUNCHPAD, WHY DON'T WE MAKE IT A ROAD TRIP?
"WE"?
YES, "WE." YOU KNOW I'VE A THING FOR MYSTERIES AND DESERTS.

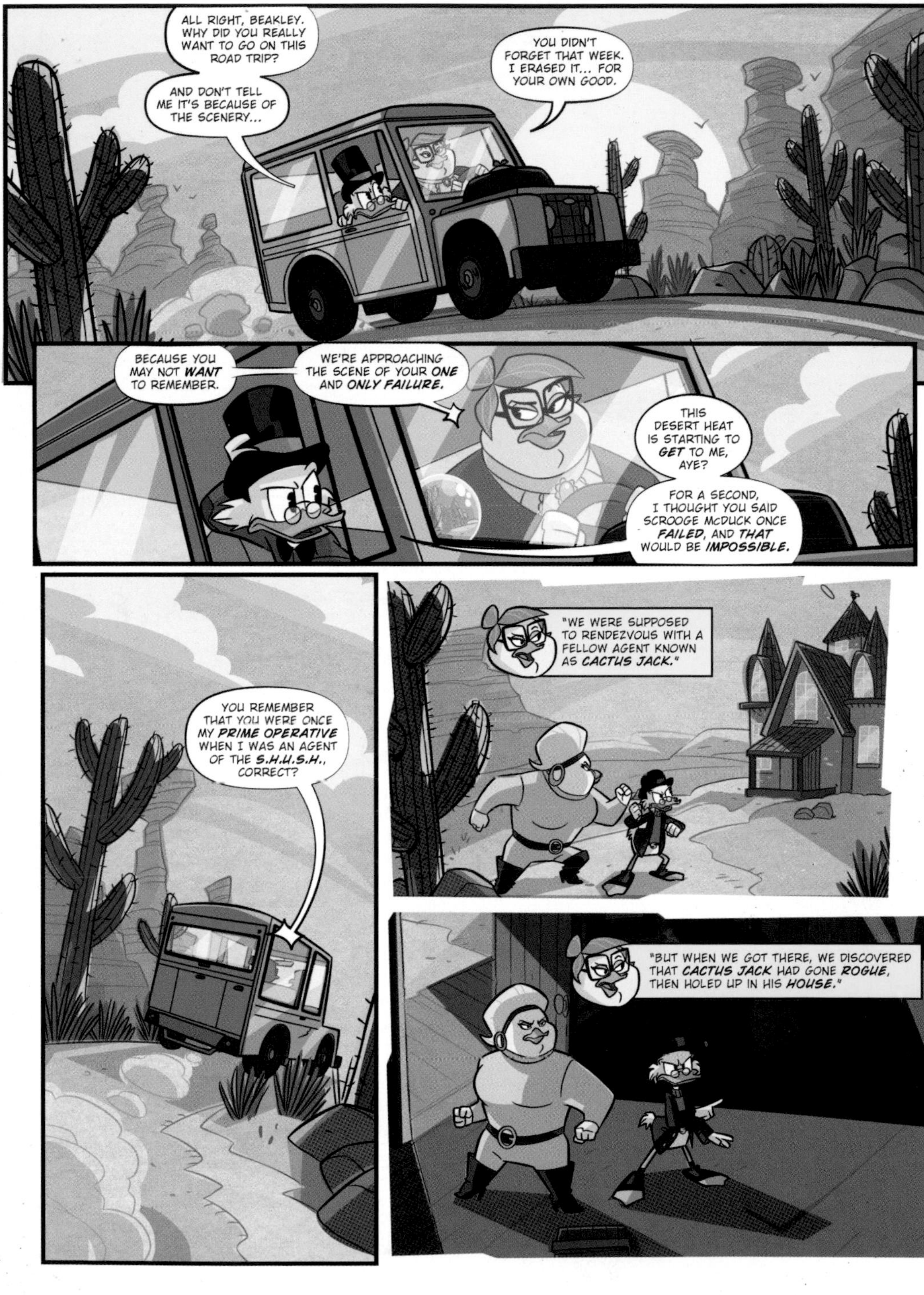
ALL RIGHT, BEAKLEY. WHY DID YOU REALLY WANT TO GO ON THIS ROAD TRIP?
AND DON'T TELL ME IT'S BECAUSE OF THE SCENERY...
YOU DIDN'T FORGET THAT WEEK. I ERASED IT... FOR YOUR OWN GOOD.
BECAUSE YOU MAY NOT WANT TO REMEMBER.
WE'RE APPROACHING THE SCENE OF YOUR ONE AND ONLY FAILURE.
THIS DESERT HEAT IS STARTING TO GET TO ME, AYE?
FOR A SECOND, I THOUGHT YOU SAID SCROOGE McDUCK ONCE FAILED, AND THAT WOULD BE IMPOSSIBLE.
YOU REMEMBER THAT YOU WERE ONCE MY PRIME OPERATIVE WHEN I WAS AN AGENT OF THE S.H.U.S.H., CORRECT?
"WE WERE SUPPOSED TO RENDEZVOUS WITH A FELLOW AGENT KNOWN AS CACTUS JACK."
"BUT WHEN WE GOT THERE, WE DISCOVERED THAT CACTUS JACK HAD GONE ROGUE, THEN HOLED UP IN HIS HOUSE."

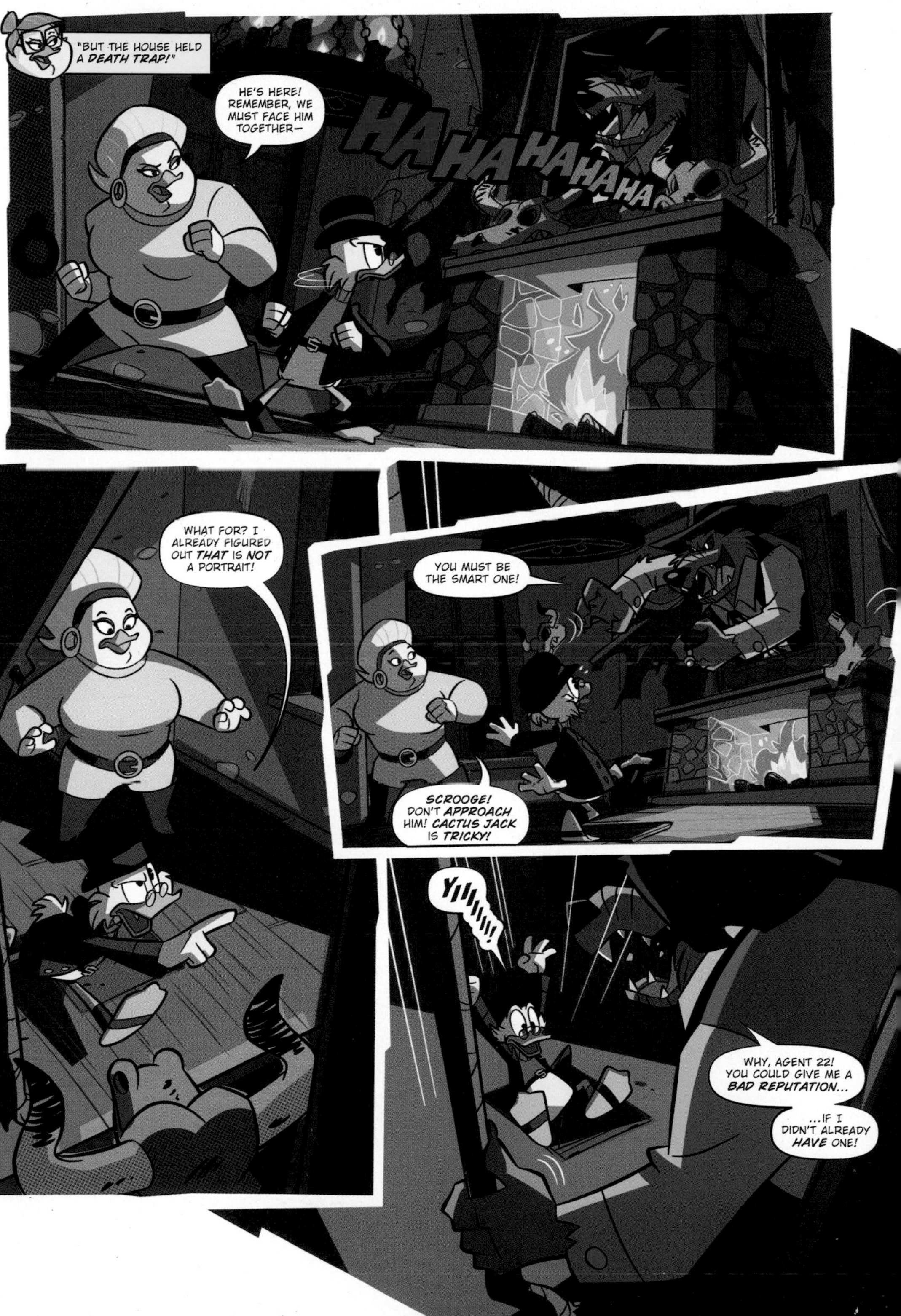
"BUT THE HOUSE HELD A DEATH TRAP!"
HE'S HERE! REMEMBER, WE MUST FACE HIM TOGETHER—
HA HA HAHAHAHA
WHAT FOR? I ALREADY FIGURED OUT THAT IS NOT A PORTRAIT!
YOU MUST BE THE SMART ONE!
SCROOGE! DON'T APPROACH HIM! CACTUS JACK IS TRICKY!
YIIIIII!
WHY, AGENT 22! YOU COULD GIVE ME A BAD REPUTATION...
...IF I DIDN'T ALREADY HAVE ONE!

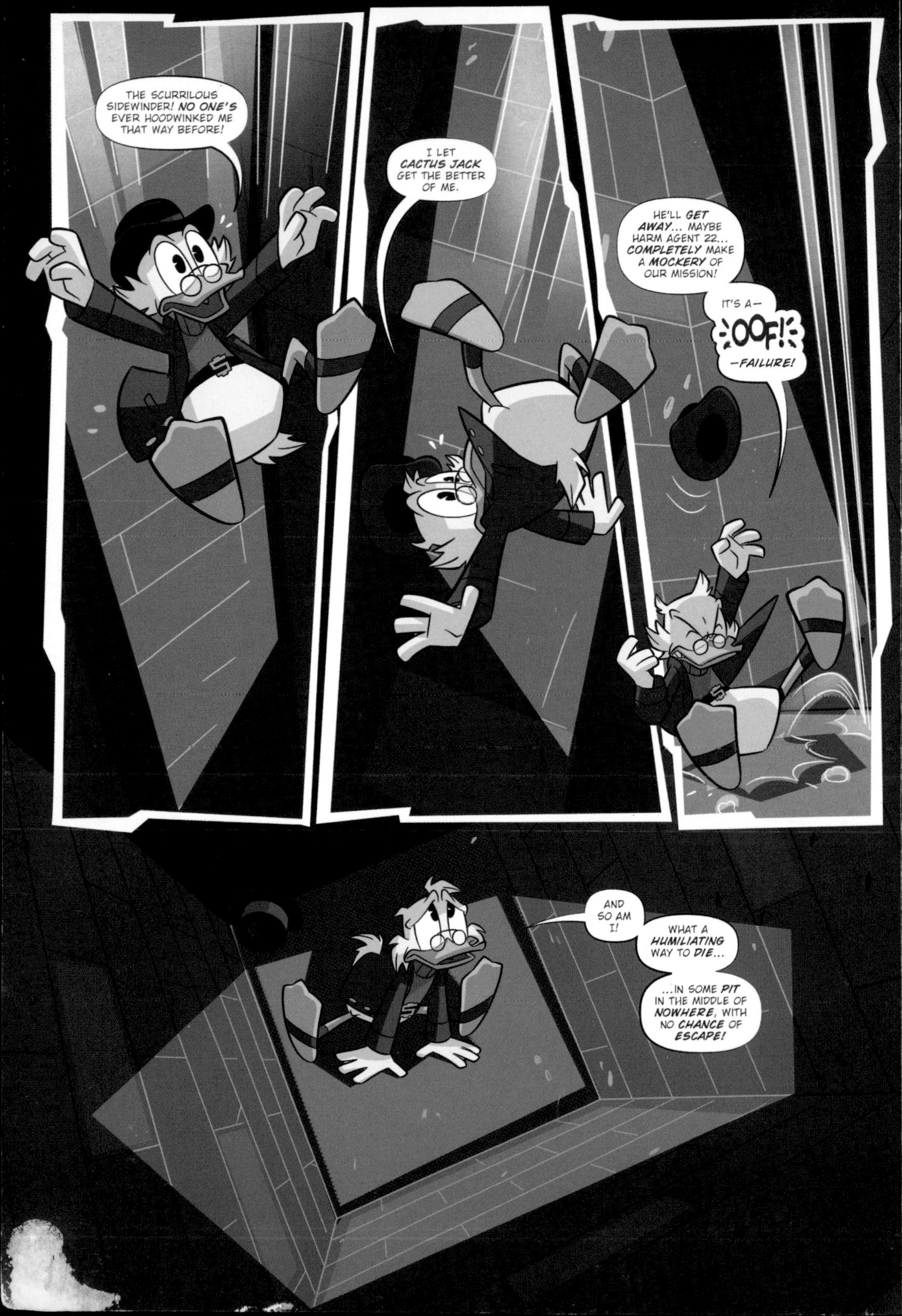

THE SCURRILOUS SIDEWINDER! NO ONE'S EVER HOODWINKED ME THAT WAY BEFORE!
I LET CACTUS JACK GET THE BETTER OF ME.
HE'LL GET AWAY... MAYBE HARM AGENT 22... COMPLETELY MAKE A MOCKERY OF OUR MISSION!
IT'S A—
OOF!
—FAILURE!
AND SO AM I!
WHAT A HUMILIATING WAY TO DIE...
...IN SOME PIT IN THE MIDDLE OF NOWHERE, WITH NO CHANCE OF ESCAPE!

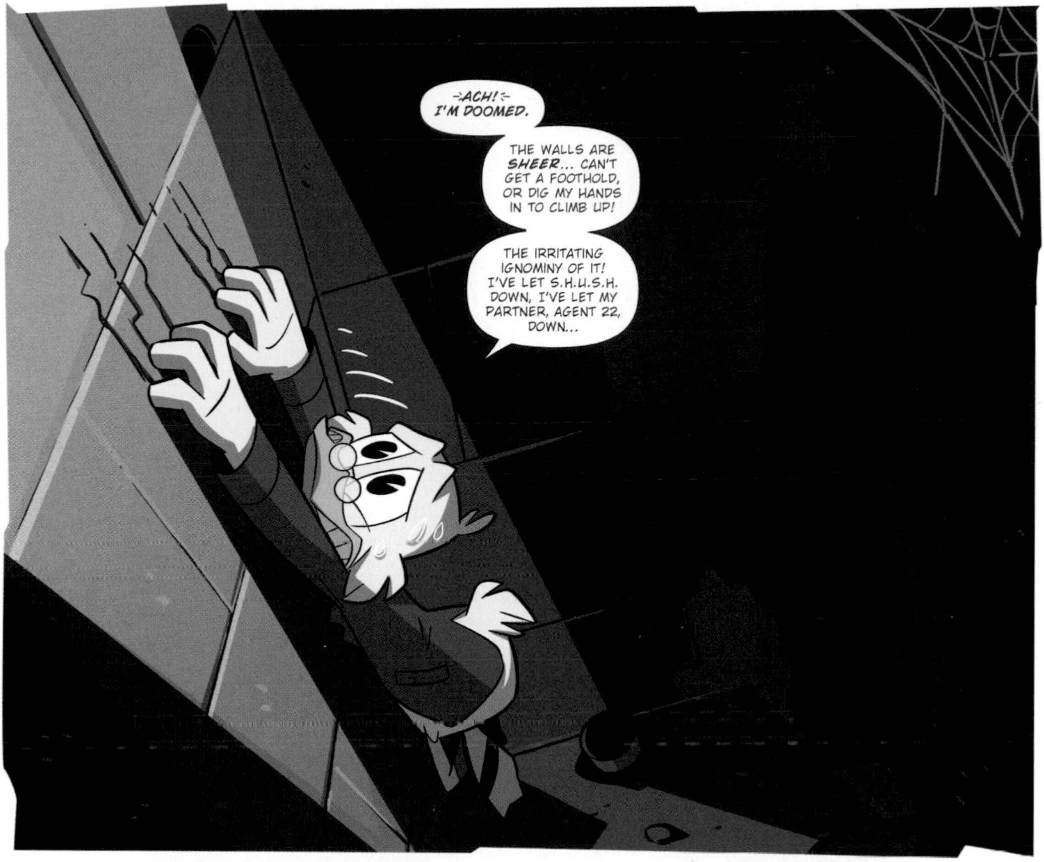
-ACH! I'M DOOMED.
THE WALLS ARE SHEER... CAN'T GET A FOOTHOLD, OR DIG MY HANDS IN TO CLIMB UP!
THE IRRITATING IGNOMINY OF IT! I'VE LET S.H.U.S.H. DOWN, I'VE LET MY PARTNER, AGENT 22, DOWN...

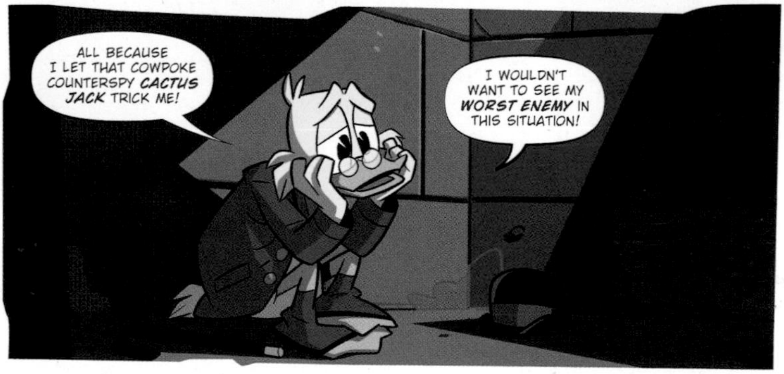
ALL BECAUSE I LET THAT COWPOKE COUNTERSPY CACTUS JACK TRICK ME!
I WOULDN'T WANT TO SEE MY WORST ENEMY IN THIS SITUATION!

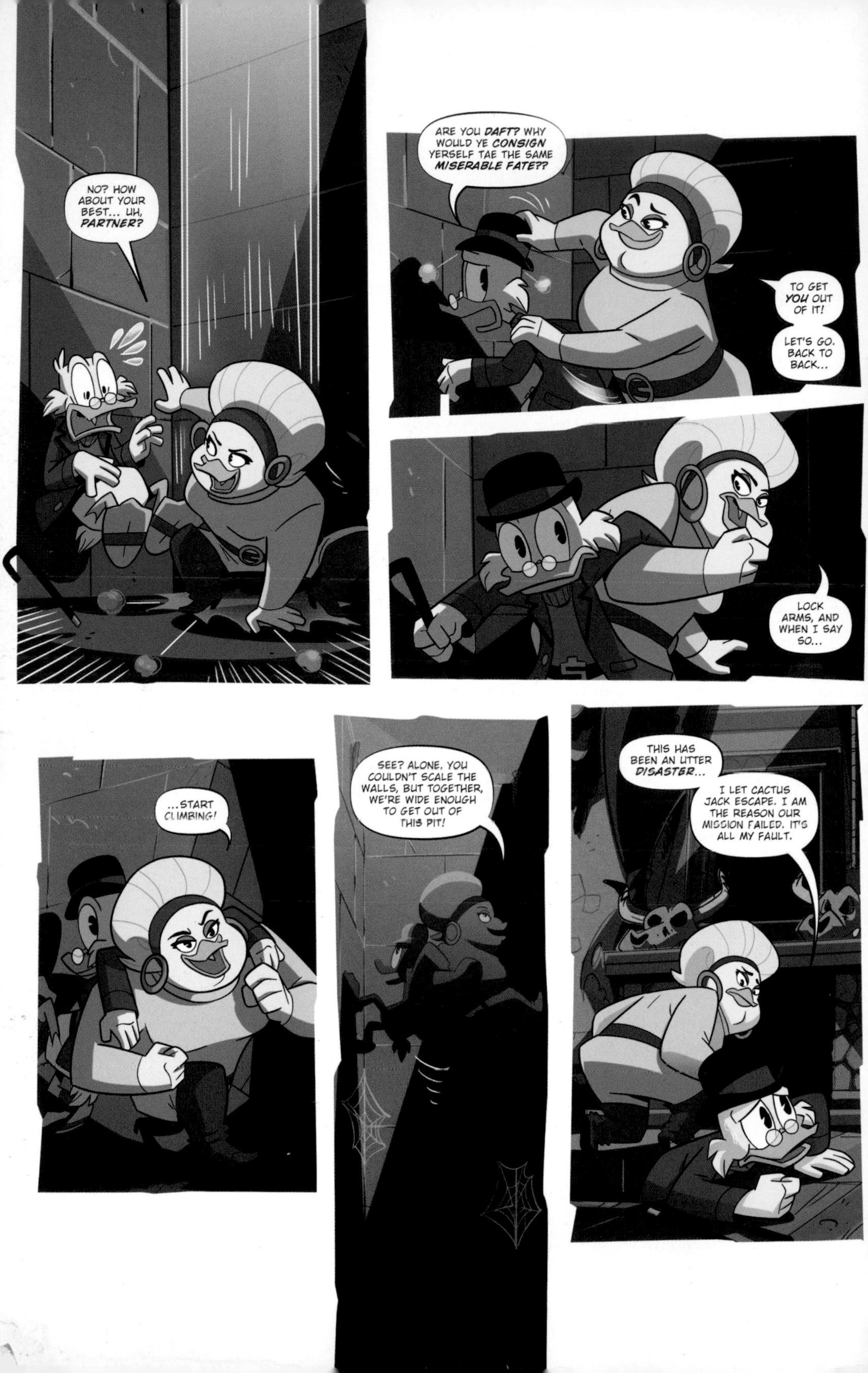
NO? HOW ABOUT YOUR BEST... UH, PARTNER?
ARE YOU DAFT? WHY WOULD YE CONSIGN YERSELF TAE THE SAME MISERABLE FATE??
TO GET YOU OUT OF IT!
LET'S GO. BACK TO BACK...
LOCK ARMS, AND WHEN I SAY SO...
...START CLIMBING!
SEE? ALONE, YOU COULDN'T SCALE THE WALLS, BUT TOGETHER, WE'RE WIDE ENOUGH TO GET OUT OF THIS PIT!
THIS HAS BEEN AN UTTER DISASTER...
I LET CACTUS JACK ESCAPE. I AM THE REASON OUR MISSION FAILED. IT'S ALL MY FAULT.

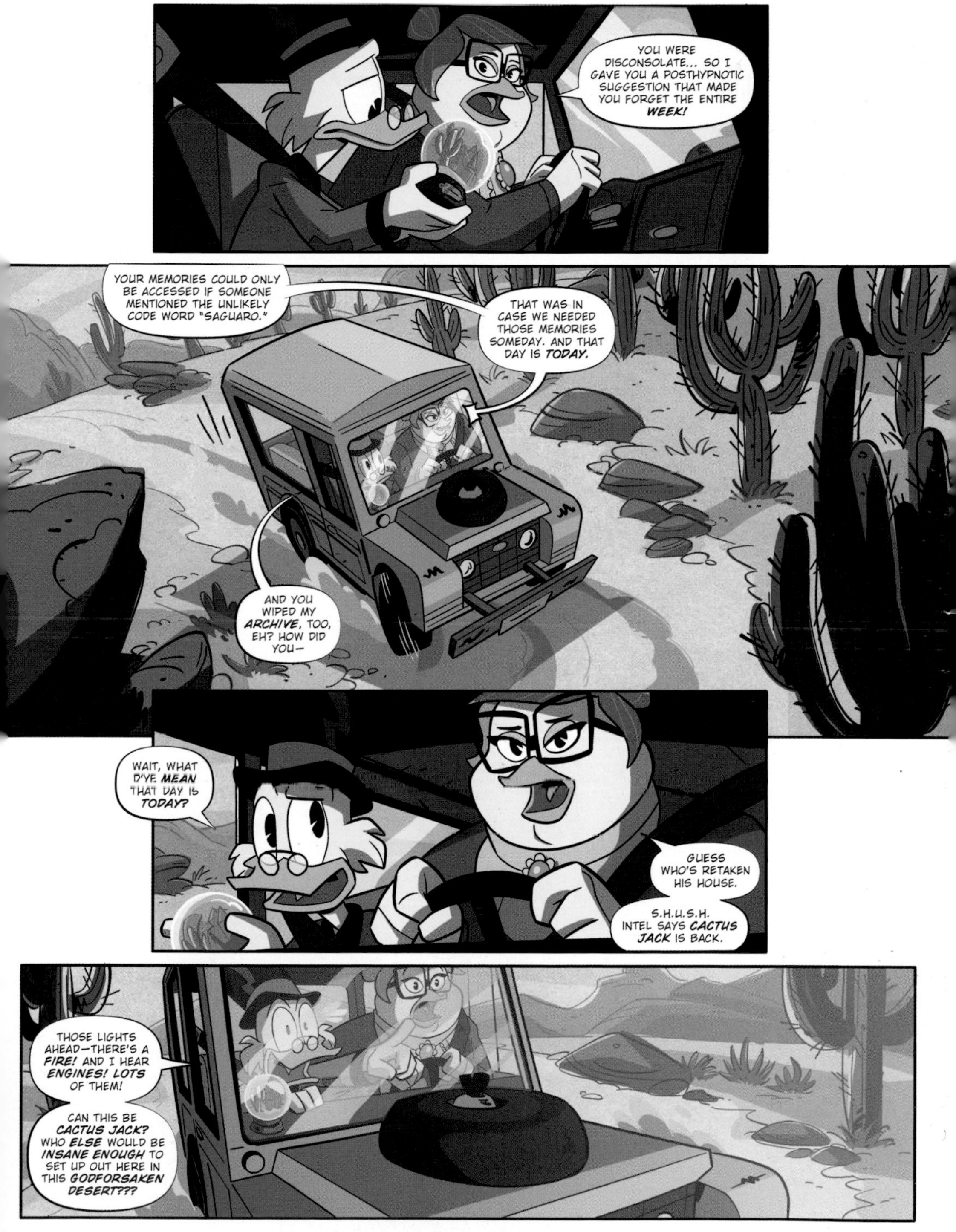
YOU WERE DISCONSOLATE... SO I GAVE YOU A POSTHYPNOTIC SUGGESTION THAT MADE YOU FORGET THE ENTIRE WEEK!
YOUR MEMORIES COULD ONLY BE ACCESSED IF SOMEONE MENTIONED THE UNLIKELY CODE WORD "SAGUARO."
THAT WAS IN CASE WE NEEDED THOSE MEMORIES SOMEDAY. AND THAT DAY IS TODAY.
AND YOU WIPED MY ARCHIVE, TOO, EH? HOW DID YOU—
WAIT, WHAT D'YE MEAN THAT DAY IS TODAY?
GUESS WHO'S RETAKEN HIS HOUSE.
S.H.U.S.H. INTEL SAYS CACTUS JACK IS BACK.
THOSE LIGHTS AHEAD—THERE'S A FIRE! AND I HEAR ENGINES! LOTS OF THEM!
CAN THIS BE CACTUS JACK? WHO ELSE WOULD BE INSANE ENOUGH TO SET UP OUT HERE IN THIS GODFORSAKEN DESERT???

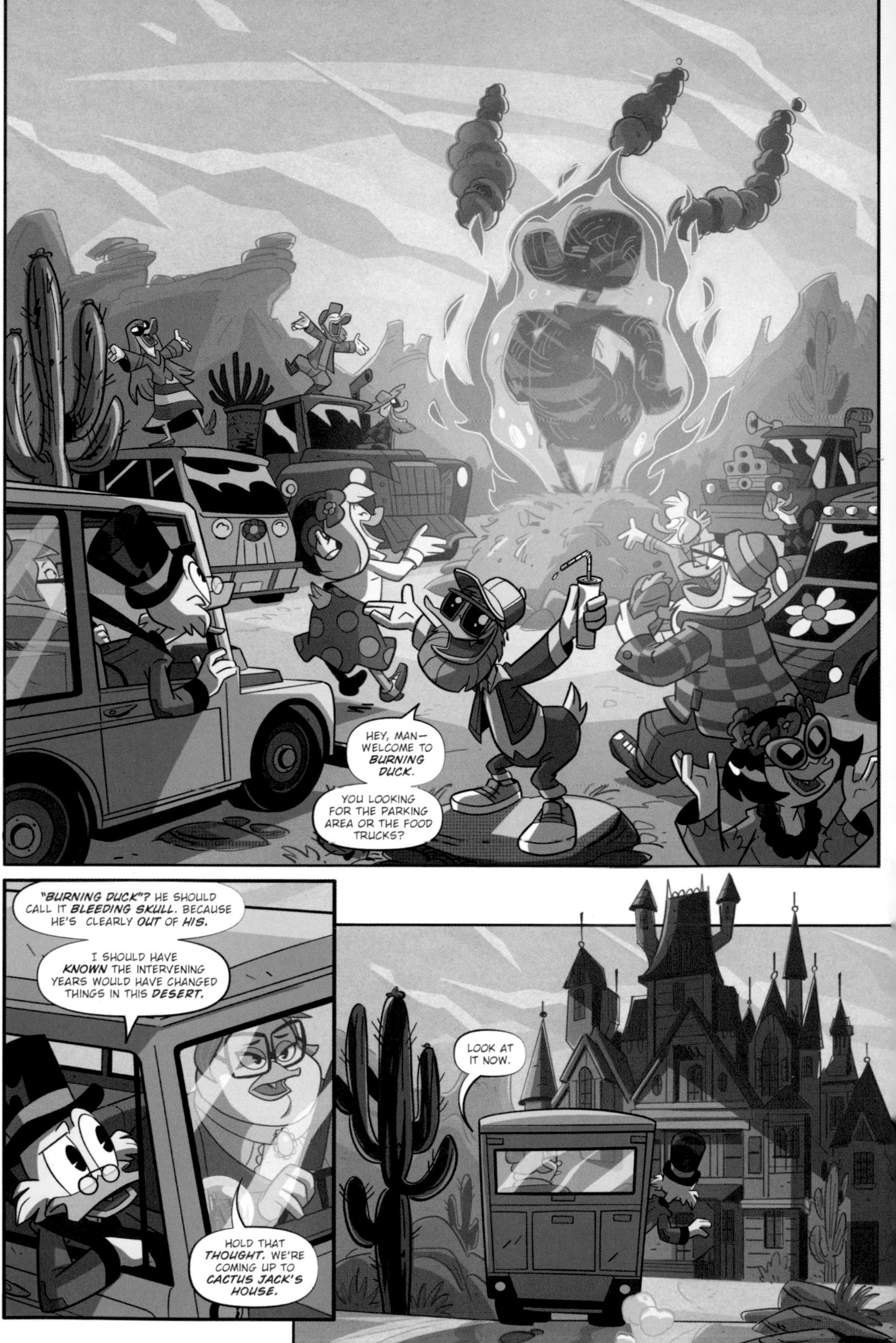
HEY, MAN— WELCOME TO BURNING DUCK.
YOU LOOKING FOR THE PARKING AREA OR THE FOOD TRUCKS?
"BURNING DUCK"? HE SHOULD CALL IT BLEEDING SKULL. BECAUSE HE'S CLEARLY OUT OF HIS.
I SHOULD HAVE KNOWN THE INTERVENING YEARS WOULD HAVE CHANGED THINGS IN THIS DESERT.
HOLD THAT THOUGHT. WE'RE COMING UP TO CACTUS JACK'S HOUSE.
LOOK AT IT NOW.

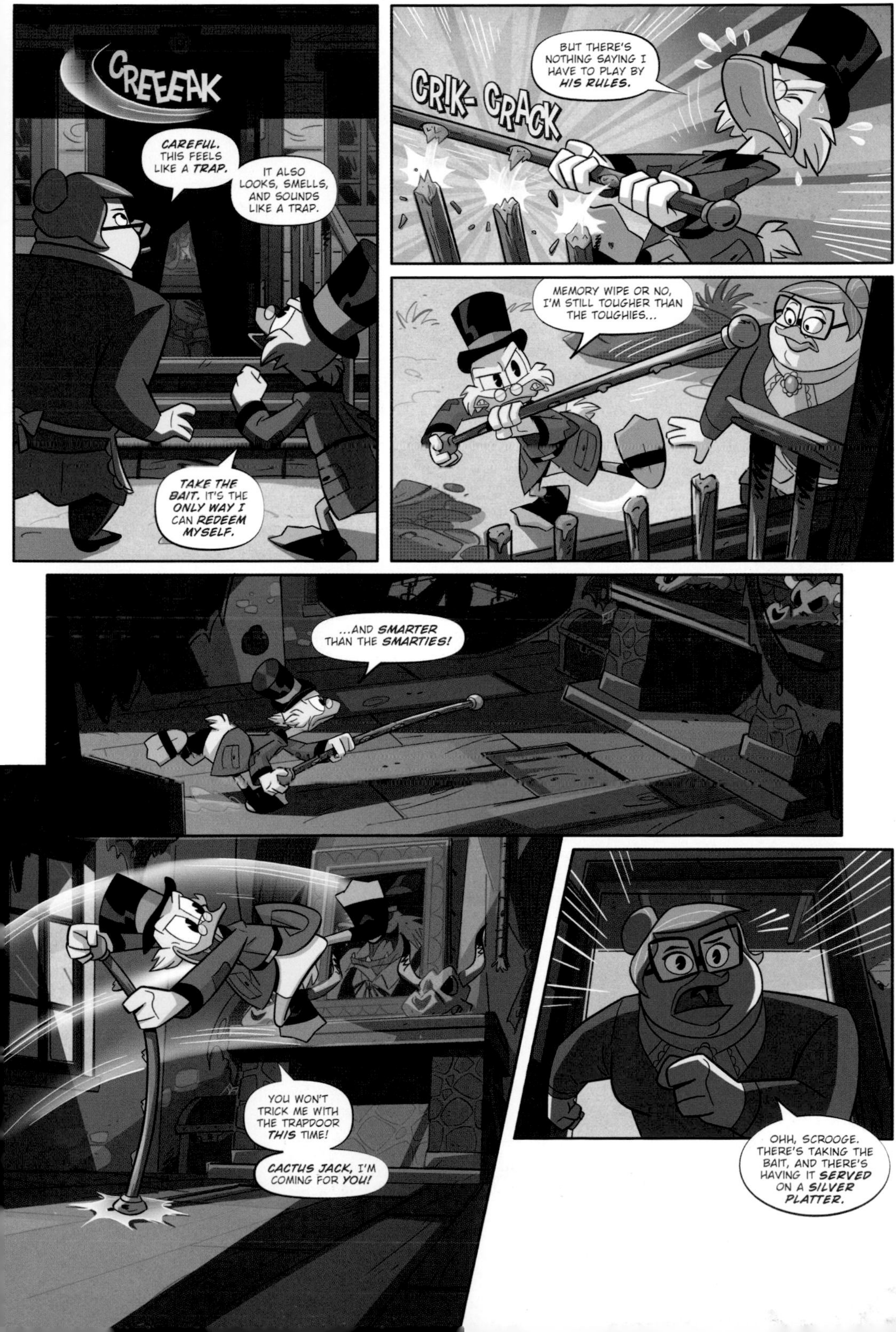
CREEEAK
CAREFUL. THIS FEELS LIKE A TRAP.
IT ALSO LOOKS, SMELLS, AND SOUNDS LIKE A TRAP.
TAKE THE BAIT. IT'S THE ONLY WAY I CAN REDEEM MYSELF.
BUT THERE'S NOTHING SAYING I HAVE TO PLAY BY HIS RULES.
CRIK- CRACK
MEMORY WIPE OR NO, I'M STILL TOUGHER THAN THE TOUGHIES...
...AND SMARTER THAN THE SMARTIES!
YOU WON'T TRICK ME WITH THE TRAPDOOR THIS TIME!
CACTUS JACK, I'M COMING FOR YOU!
OHH, SCROOGE. THERE'S TAKING THE BAIT, AND THERE'S HAVING IT SERVED ON A SILVER PLATTER.

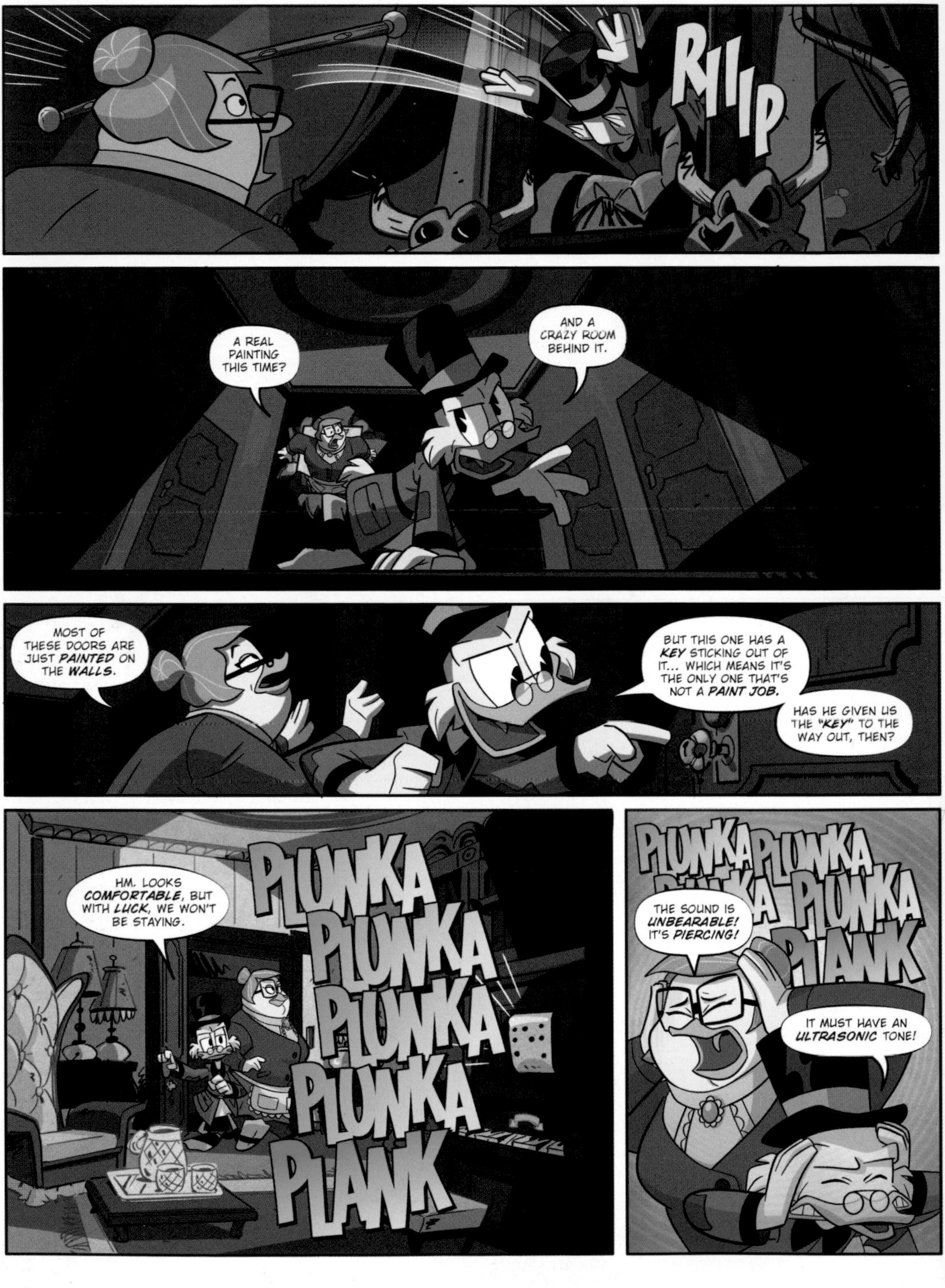
RIIIP
A REAL PAINTING THIS TIME?
AND A CRAZY ROOM BEHIND IT.
MOST OF THESE DOORS ARE JUST *PAINTED* ON THE *WALLS*.
BUT THIS ONE HAS A *KEY* STICKING OUT OF IT... WHICH MEANS IT'S THE ONLY ONE THAT'S NOT A *PAINT JOB.*
HAS HE GIVEN US THE *"KEY"* TO THE WAY OUT, THEN?
HM. LOOKS *COMFORTABLE*, BUT WITH *LUCK*, WE WON'T BE STAYING.
PLUNKA PLUNKA PLUNKA PLUNKA PLANK
PLUNKA PLUNKA PLUNKA PLUNKA PLANK
THE SOUND IS *UNBEARABLE!* IT'S *PIERCING!*
IT MUST HAVE AN *ULTRASONIC* TONE!

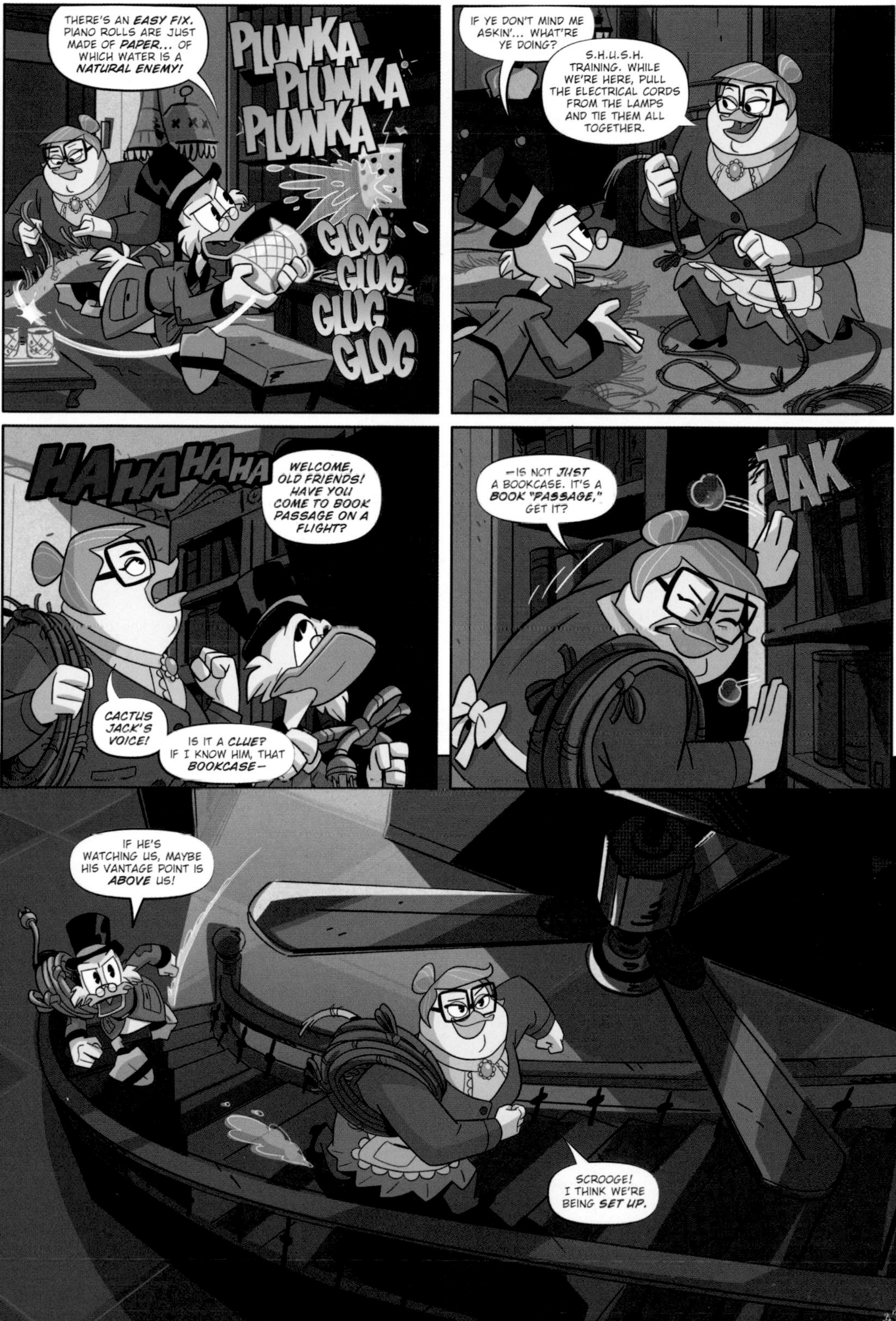
THERE'S AN EASY FIX. PIANO ROLLS ARE JUST MADE OF PAPER... OF WHICH WATER IS A NATURAL ENEMY!
PLUNKA PLUNKA PLUNKA
GLOG GLUG GLUG GLOG
IF YE DON'T MIND ME ASKIN'... WHAT'RE YE DOING?
S.H.U.S.H. TRAINING. WHILE WE'RE HERE, PULL THE ELECTRICAL CORDS FROM THE LAMPS AND TIE THEM ALL TOGETHER.
HAHAHAHAHA
WELCOME, OLD FRIENDS! HAVE YOU COME TO BOOK PASSAGE ON A FLIGHT?
CACTUS JACK'S VOICE!
IS IT A CLUE? IF I KNOW HIM, THAT BOOKCASE—
—IS NOT JUST A BOOKCASE. IT'S A BOOK "PASSAGE," GET IT?
TAK
IF HE'S WATCHING US, MAYBE HIS VANTAGE POINT IS ABOVE US!
SCROOGE! I THINK WE'RE BEING SET UP.

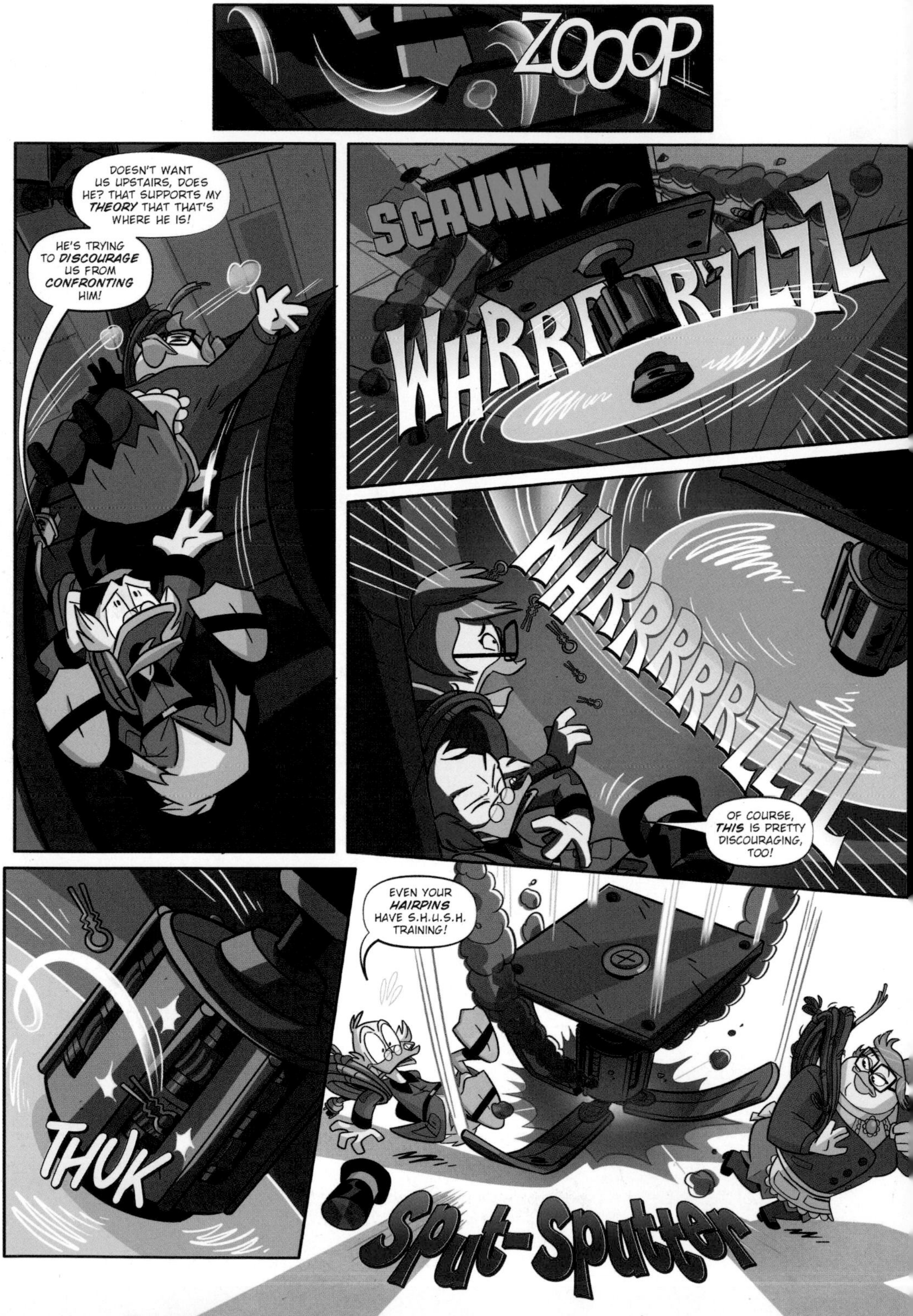
ZOOOP
DOESN'T WANT US UPSTAIRS, DOES HE? THAT SUPPORTS MY THEORY THAT THAT'S WHERE HE IS!
HE'S TRYING TO DISCOURAGE US FROM CONFRONTING HIM!
SCRUNK
WHRRRRRZZZZ
WHRRRRRRRRZZZZ
OF COURSE, THIS IS PRETTY DISCOURAGING, TOO!
THUK
EVEN YOUR HAIRPINS HAVE S.H.U.S.H. TRAINING!
Sput-Sputter

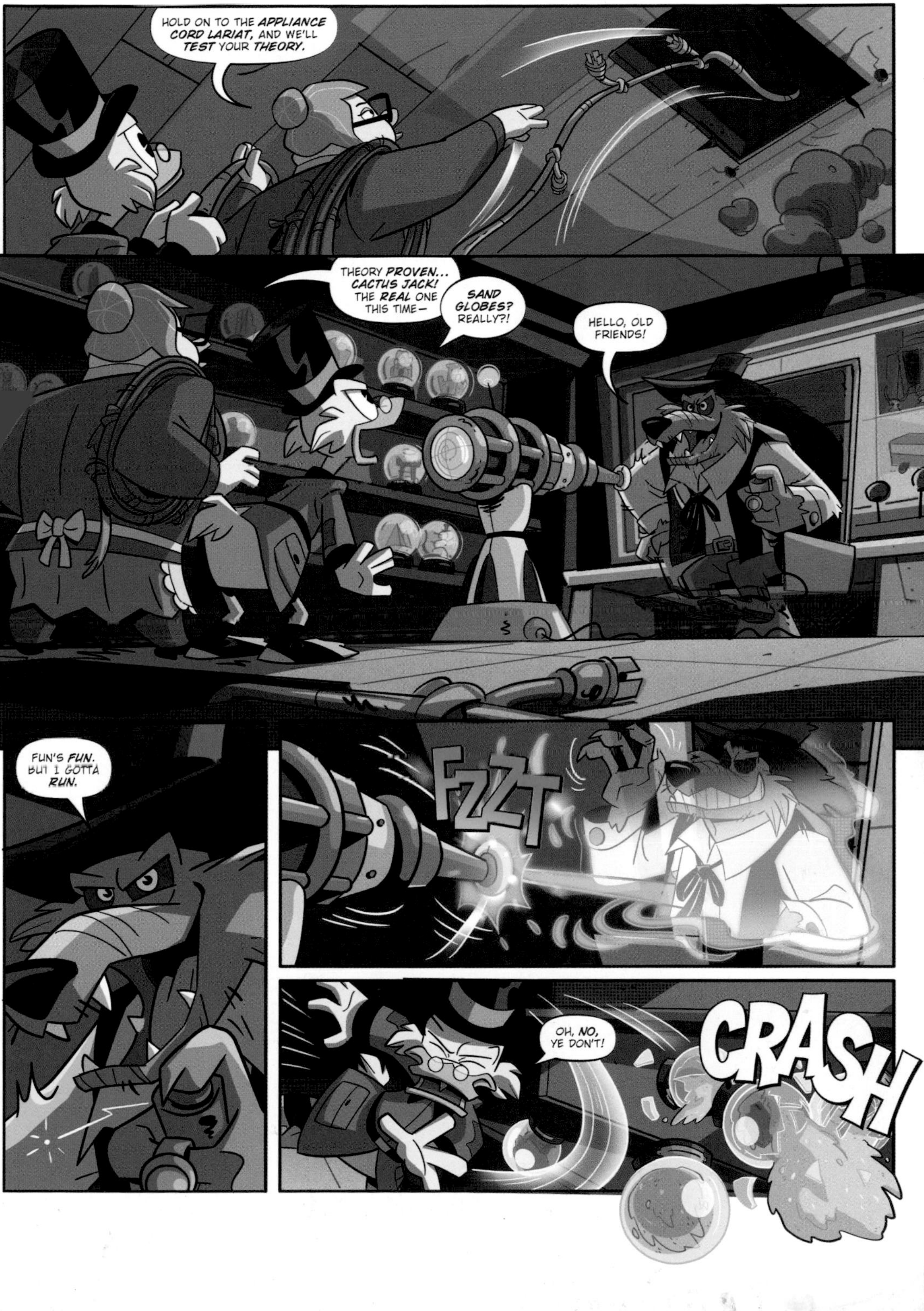
HOLD ON TO THE APPLIANCE CORD LARIAT, AND WE'LL TEST YOUR THEORY.
THEORY PROVEN... CACTUS JACK! THE REAL ONE THIS TIME—
SAND GLOBES? REALLY?!
HELLO, OLD FRIENDS!
FUN'S FUN. BUT I GOTTA RUN.
FZZZT
OH, NO, YE DON'T!
CRASH

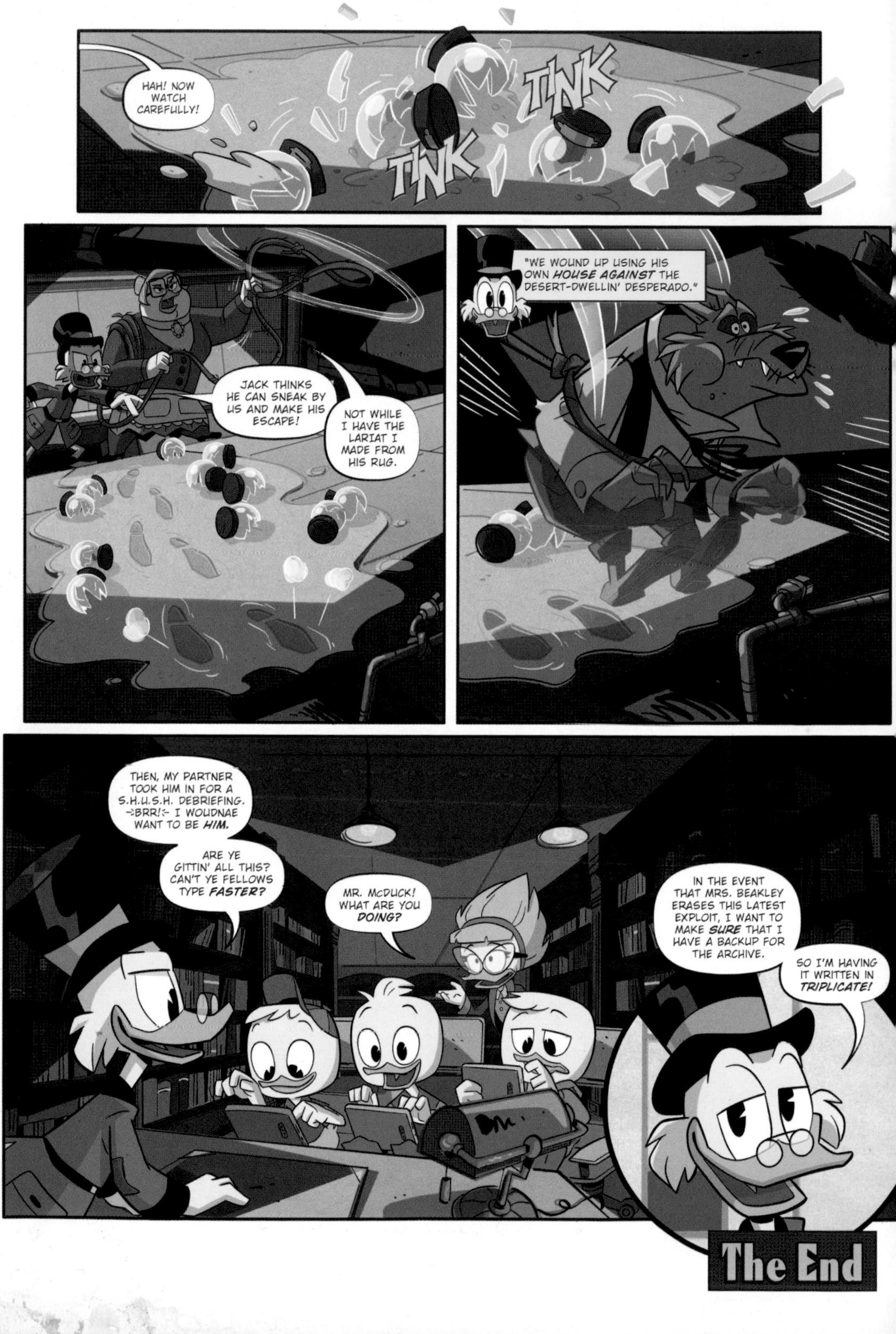
HAH! NOW WATCH CAREFULLY!
TINK
TINK
JACK THINKS HE CAN SNEAK BY US AND MAKE HIS ESCAPE!
NOT WHILE I HAVE THE LARIAT I MADE FROM HIS RUG.
"WE WOUND UP USING HIS OWN HOUSE AGAINST THE DESERT-DWELLIN' DESPERADO."
THEN, MY PARTNER TOOK HIM IN FOR A S.H.U.S.H. DEBRIEFING. -BRR!- I WOUDNAE WANT TO BE HIM.
ARE YE GITTIN' ALL THIS? CAN'T YE FELLOWS TYPE FASTER?
MR. McDUCK! WHAT ARE YOU DOING?
IN THE EVENT THAT MRS. BEAKLEY ERASES THIS LATEST EXPLOIT, I WANT TO MAKE SURE THAT I HAVE A BACKUP FOR THE ARCHIVE.
SO I'M HAVING IT WRITTEN IN TRIPLICATE!
The End

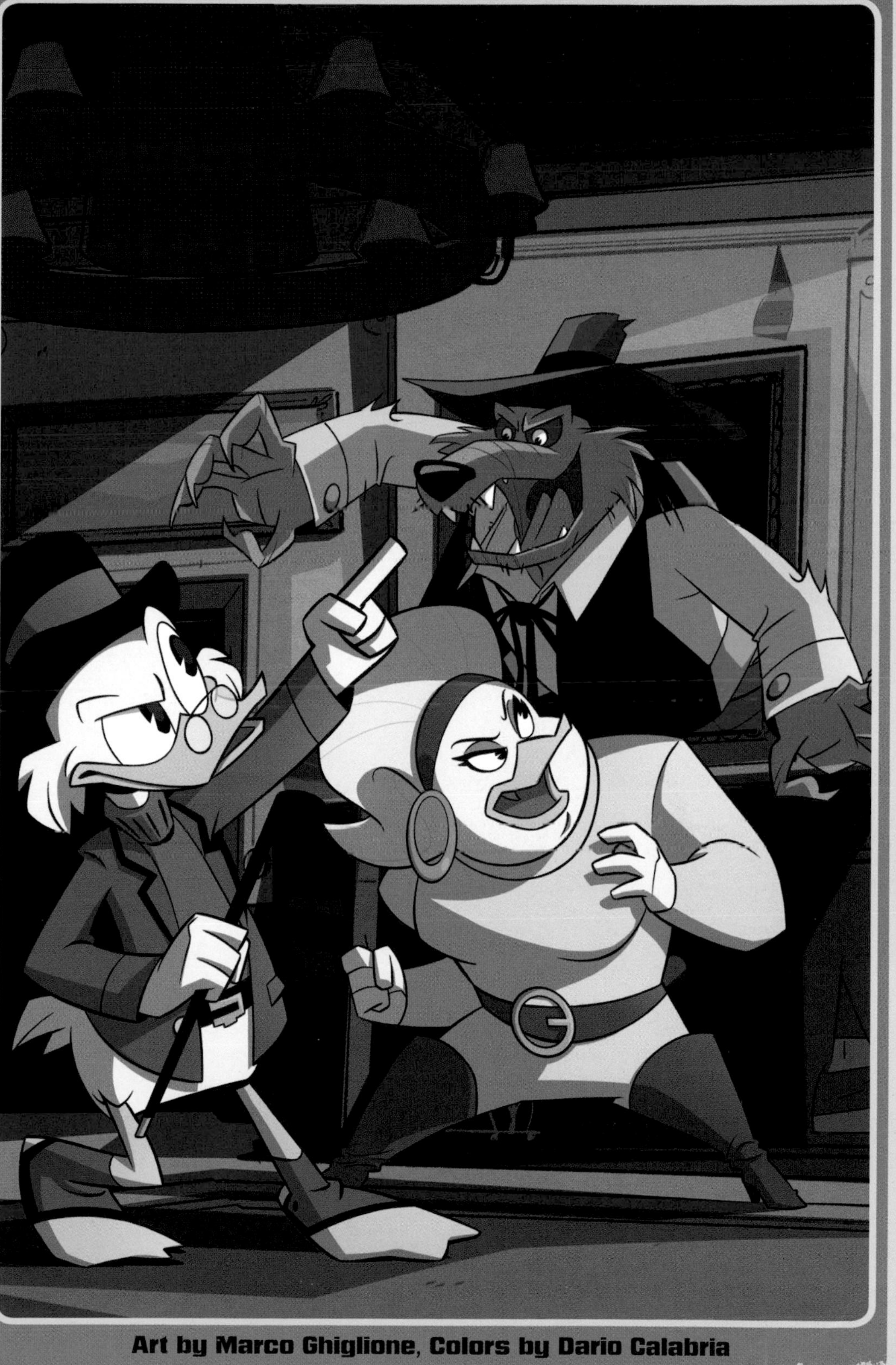

Art by Marco Ghiglione, Colors by Dario Calabria

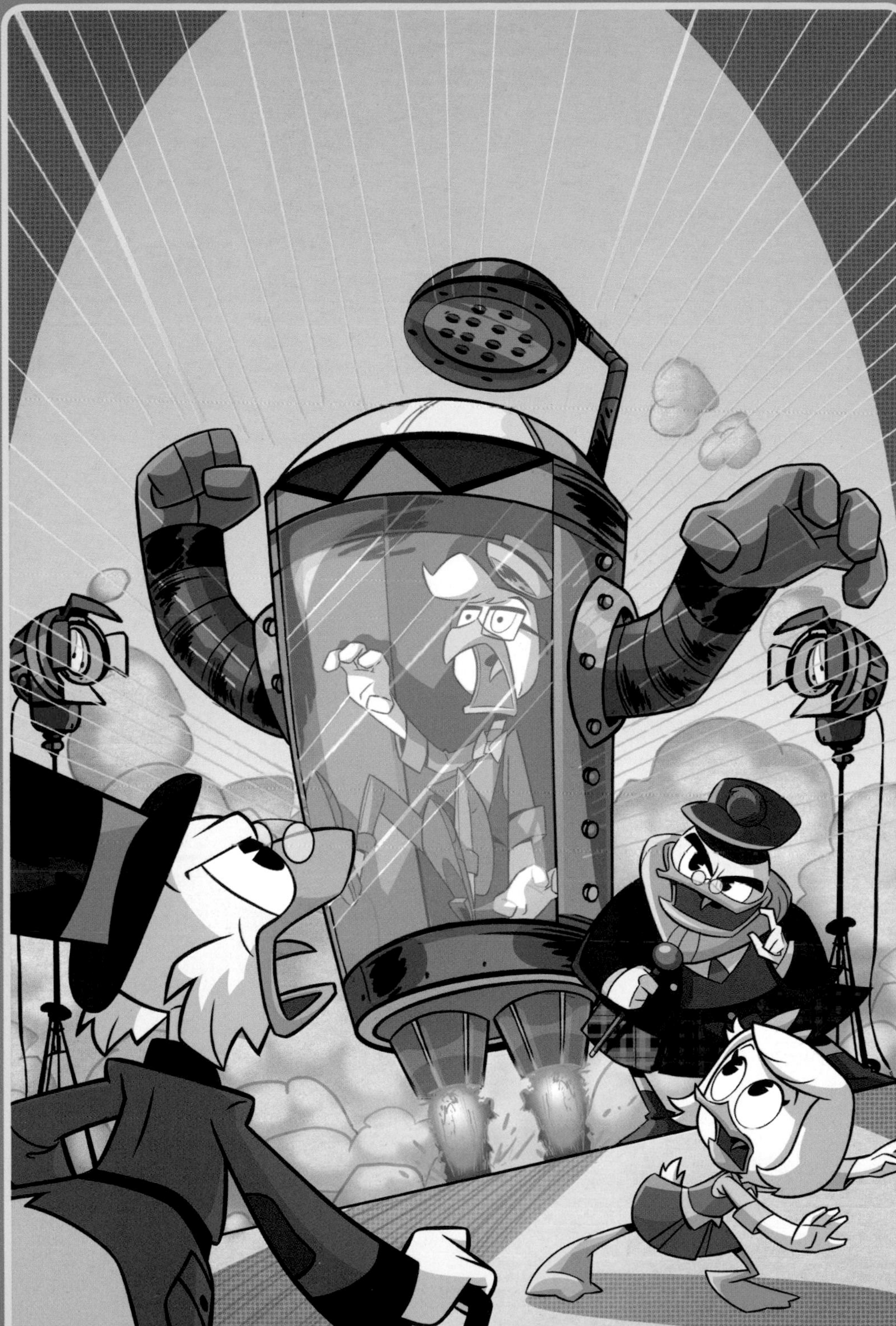

Art by Marco Ghiglione, Colors by Lucio De Giuseppe

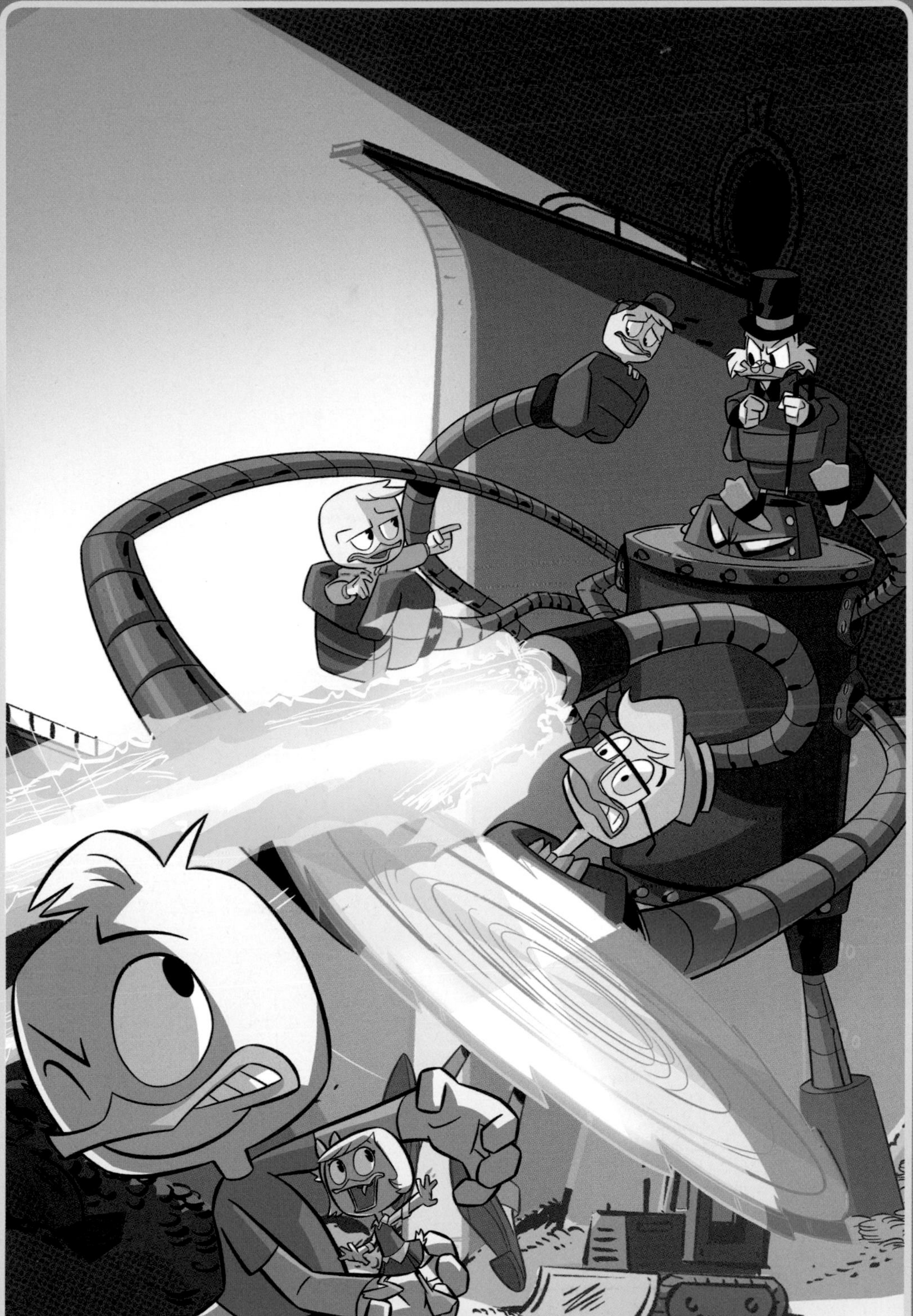

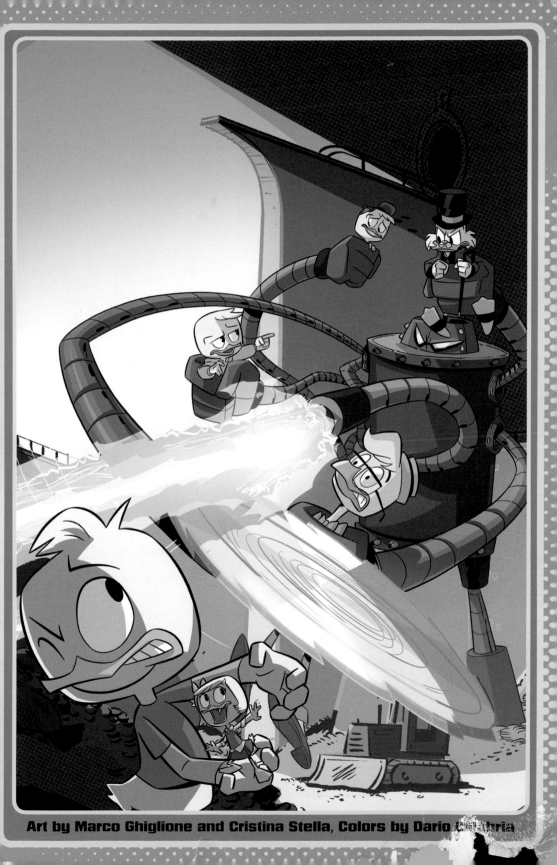

Art by Marco Ghiglione and Cristina Stella, Colors by Dario C[illegible]bria

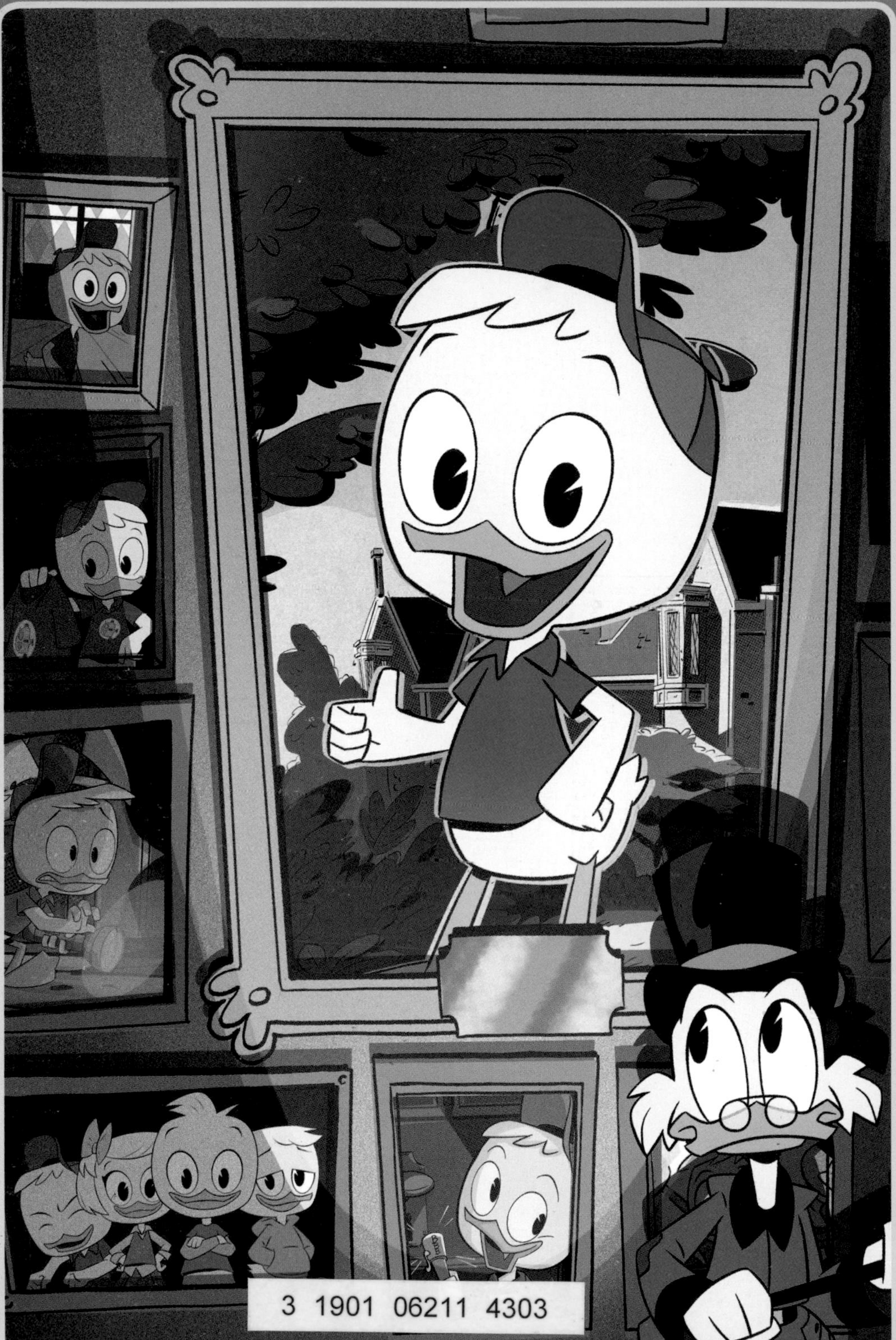

Art by DuckTales Creative Team